Following a nine-year-long career serving as a merchant navy deck officer, Peter Muller dedicated the following twenty-eight years of his working life to public service. After opting for early retirement, Peter has been able to concentrate on a variety of activities including fishing, astronomy and playing the accordion.

Farewell Chapelon is Peter Muller's first novel.

To the generations who ‘manned the whips’, in practice – and in anger. Their combined efforts saved over 24,000 lives.

Peter Muller

FAREWELL CHAPELON

AUSTIN MACAULEY PUBLISHERS™
LONDON • CAMBRIDGE • NEW YORK • SHARJAH

A CIP catalogue record for this title is available from the British Library.

ISBN 9781398436640 (Paperback)
ISBN 9781398436657 (ePub e-book)

www.austinmacauley.com

First Published 2022
Austin Macauley Publishers Ltd®
1 Canada Square
Canary Wharf
London
E14 5AA

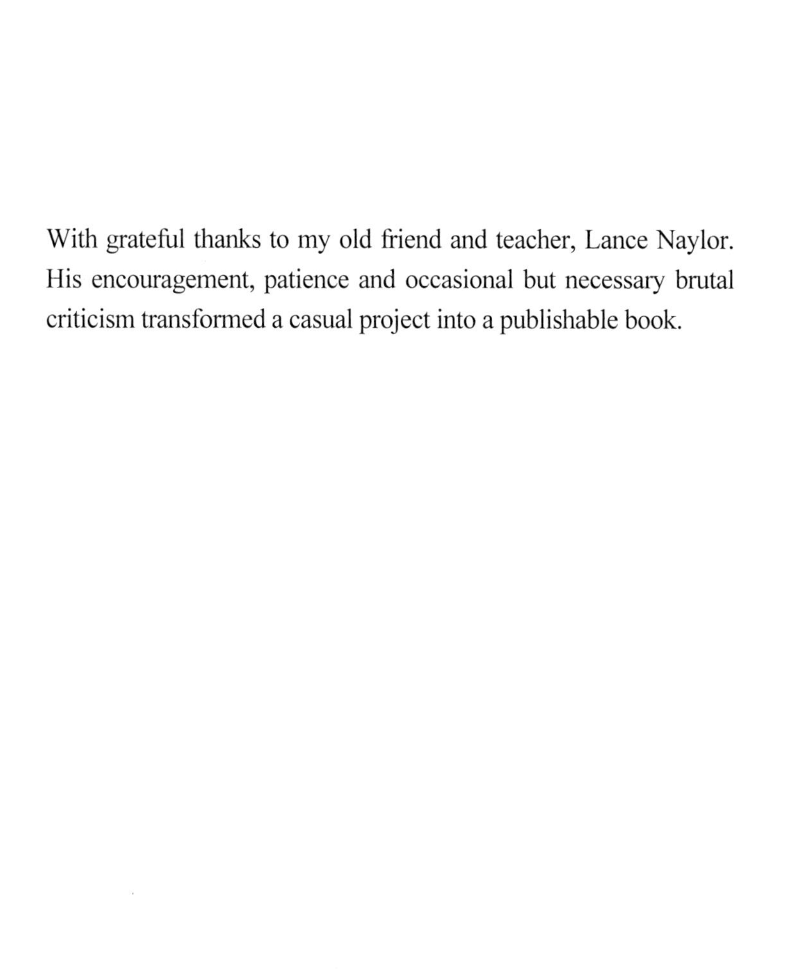

With grateful thanks to my old friend and teacher, Lance Naylor. His encouragement, patience and occasional but necessary brutal criticism transformed a casual project into a publishable book.

Chapter 1
Departure

Seeking fresh air Chapelon's master slid open the wheelhouse door. He felt the icy blast from a near gale as he strode out onto the starboard bridge wing. As well as trying to conceal his dark mood from his crew as they prepared their ship for departure, he was also relieved to escape the confines of his office, situated within the decks beneath his feet. The frenzied routine of completing ship's business after receiving orders for an unexpected and rushed sailing had been enough of a task on its own. Then he learned about a problem with the third engineer.

He was grateful the chief engineer had effectively dealt with it. The blazing row between the third and his wife had reverberated across the engineers' alleyway. To all accounts the chief had even felt the need to take their six-year-old daughter into his state room and entertained her while the argument exploded and the accusations between both had been vicious. The chief had then discreetly interrupted the master as he was signing a note of protest for their agent who was sat opposite him. Trying to defend his engineering officer, the chief remarked he was an expert at his job, before muttering about the stupidity of being married when you worked on a ship. Feeling somewhat brow beaten with this additional problem, the master had been surprised when shortly afterwards the third had knocked on his door and determinedly stated his family would remain on board for their forthcoming coastal passage.

The master now allowed his eyes to scan a cold, leaden sky, turbulent with foreboding. What he saw and mentally digested made him briefly frown. From his lofty, open position he was also able to survey the well-worn and none too clean wharf below him, against which his ship snugged. Godown doors were tight shut against a rising, biting wind. Within the vast warehouses and storage spaces, stevedores and riggers sheltered from the frigid weather, partaking as best they could of their two-hours lunch break.

The scene around him portrayed a colourless, near desolate world. It simply added to the general air of sullen depression that he felt surrounded him.

Mooring gangs were sulkily busy though, annoyed at having had their own meal break disturbed. They hunched their bodies against the deteriorating weather, heaving eyes belonging to the ship's ropes off bollards dotted along the wharf. As his own roving eyes glanced past the wheelhouse front towards the port side, the master noted that a pair of small, powerful tugs were nosing across the sheltered basin, ready to aid his ship with her undocking. He quietly, almost plaintively wished he could have caught a last glimpse of the City of Dunkirk, resplendent and cheerful in its Christmas decorations and lights.

The monotonous acres of drab warehouses, cranes, stacked containers and tank farms denied him even that. Such was the life of a mariner.

He was at a personal career pinnacle, with over thirty-five years of professional seafaring behind him. Along the way he had gained a well-respected and trusted reputation. As a ship's master his competence was beyond question: a captain qualified and able to command any ship, anywhere in the world. And yet…as his hair grew greyer and his skin became more lined and weather beaten, his recent thoughts had increasingly become entangled with the personal costs of his chosen career, despite its interesting professional challenges and massive financial rewards. His children had already grown into young adults with him barely realising what had happened. For that matter he had never really got to know or understand them either. That fact had suddenly struck him like a hammer blow during his last period of leave. The youngsters were almost remote strangers, while his wife, who had learned to tolerate months of separation as the downside of being wed to a mariner, had got used to managing virtually everything on her own. He now hardly dared interfere or comment about their, or more correctly, her arrangements for maintaining their domestic affairs. It had to be that way. Now, increasingly when home on leave, the first two weeks were always wonderful. After that, he had effectively become a spare part within his own household. Returning to his ship, where he commanded recognition and respect and where he could genuinely feel useful had become a positive relief. *And what of retirement?* he wondered. It was only a few years away. The mere thought filled him with dread.

For all of his domestic shortcomings, he still quietly reflected that perhaps, just for once, it would have been wonderful for his family to join him on his ship for Christmas.

His eyes focused on the forecastle, where the clatter of the ship's windlass broke into his thoughts. The mate and his team worked reluctantly but efficiently as they singled the lines up to a breast rope and a back spring. Up there, they were fully exposed to the near gale that was blowing. Now, as he stepped out to the end of the starboard bridge wing, the master or 'Old Man', as he was more informally known, gazed aft where a mooring line slid into the cold, black and greasy water of their dock basin. It created gentle ripples as it snaked across the void between ship and jetty before rising dripping onto the poop. Unwilling hands, numbed with cold worked the line on a mooring winch drum as the massive, platted mooring rope was retrieved and coiled on deck. Despite their own despondency and disappointment, the after crew were working efficiently too, under the watchful eye of the second mate, as they singled up to a back spring and stern rope.

The master's assessment about the threatening sky was proved to be spot on. A wind driven sleet flurry saw him seek the sanctuary of his wheelhouse just in time to greet the arrival of their harbour pilot who was being escorted by their nervous first trip cadet.

Both were numbed and pinched with cold, while the cadet's uniform still bore an overall look of newness.

With Christmas now only two days away, it had seemed an impossible dream that the ship would be alongside, in her home port of Dunkirk for the special festival.

Everybody was delighted and excited as arrangements were made for loved ones to join Chapelon's crew in her comfortable accommodation. Even the galley had got ready to go into overdrive to make it a memorable occasion.

That was before their expectations were instantly shattered. The owner's agent suddenly arrived with their new orders. They directed the ship to sail immediately for Grangemouth. A special cargo commanding premium freight rates had arrived from Scandinavia and following its Scottish transhipment port, it was destined for Abidjan and Monrovia. Grangemouth would now be their last port of call, prior to over two months of not particularly pleasant coasting around West Africa. Christmas would almost certainly be just another routine working day for his ship. The master keenly felt and shared his crew's frustration and disappointment but dared not show it. He, and he alone was the owner's legal representative – and the commercial efficiency of the ship and her owner's bidding constantly prevailed upon his shoulders.

It still did not stop his professional commitments and responsibilities being overridden by a feeling of gut-wrenching despair when he had telephoned his wife and family at their home near Caen. He felt himself stammer as he made the unhappy announcement they would no longer be joining him on his ship for Christmas. Oh they had made all the correct, sympathetic noises as he spoke, but did he also detect a slight feeling of relief, now they could continue with their own plans for the festive season? He briefly shook his head. French nationals to the last man, many of his crew had been obliged to make similar calls to their expectant loved ones. The third engineer's wife and young daughter had of course already arrived on board. Then, following the row that had been heard by many, they had totally surprised him with their decision to stay for the coastal voyage to Grangemouth. Even before that altercation in their cabin, he had earlier watched the third engineer greet their arrival at the gangway.

Chapelon's captain had immediately gained a first impression of unease between them as the third helped carry his family's baggage on board. At least, the captain thankfully reflected, his own family was well adapted to surviving the ordeal of his career. Being married to a mariner could be a tough undertaking.

With severe gales forecast in the North Sea, the master scornfully and with some cruelty and sarcasm in his reeling thoughts, hoped the mother and child would enjoy the trip before dismissing them totally from his mind as his ship made ready to sail.

"Bonjour." The master's response to the pilot's greeting was automatic.

On the outboard side of the wheelhouse windows heavy duty, horizontal wipers seemed to be groaning against the weight of wind and sleet that was now turning to snow and ice as it hammered against their reinforced glass, reducing visibility to near zero. The misery of the crew on the exposed decks below was almost tangible, particularly for a pair who had been despatched to make a tug fast alongside the main deck in front of his lofty perch.

The frozen first trip cadet had been sent over to a corner behind the chart console towards the rear of the wheelhouse to make coffee. It could have been an act of kindness as the teenager inwardly questioned the wisdom of embarking on such an unusual and at present awful career. The scrunched-up isobars on a weather-fax and an accompanying abysmal forecast made him realise that a couple of days of seasickness and discomfort would be his lot!

The master and pilot rapidly and readily agreed to wait a few minutes until the worst of the squall had passed before undocking. Out on deck, forward and aft, the crew were trying to seek any available shelter as they huddled against bulkheads and deck houses. The team on the bridge meanwhile, despite their grimness and disappointment was efficiently ready in all respects. A helmsman patiently waited at the small ship's wheel that jutted out from an Arkus autopilot. Both radars maintained their monotonous sweeps with their daylight viewing hoods in place over their circular, cathode-ray tube screens.

Compass repeaters quietly clicked away in response to the master gyro compass, snugged safely away in a compartment next to the chart console. At the control desk for the main engine stood the senior cadet, eyes scanning the indicator lights and illuminated buttons in front of him. The main engine was on 'standby'. The bridge had direct command of the ship's means of propulsion. He quickly double checked that the ratchet pawls were disengaged from the combined bridge telegraph / throttle lever on which his hands lightly rested. It controlled a massive Sulzer Diesel engine silent and slumbering, hidden deep below his feet in the ship's hull. An air pressure gauge conveniently placed next to the throttle confirmed that two long, cylindrical, compressed air reservoirs, mounted halfway up the port-side of the engine room were fully topped up. Their potential energy would provide the impetus to get the ship's main engine turning when the time to leave came. Draped in heavy weather gear, the second helmsman was designated bridge lookout. The third mate wore over his white shirt and black tie a thick, navy-blue pullover fitted with epaulettes. With binoculars swinging around his neck he quietly made a final check of the chart console before walking around to the wheelhouse front, bridge movement book and pen in his hand. The bridge was fully prepared and ready in all respects for Chapelon's departure. The master instinctively knew there was no need to ask for confirmation. While it was obvious that all his crew, with the one inevitable exception of the ship's chief engineer were upset about leaving Dunkirk before Christmas, they were at the same time reliable professionals and there was now a job to contemplate.

For a brief moment the master let his thoughts secretly focus on his young third officer as he quietly went about his duties. The deck officer's features and expression fully hid any hint about his inner feelings from scrutiny. *Had he once been like that?* the master wondered. Would this reliable and pleasant young man make the sea a lifelong career? His attitude and professionalism were beyond reproach. Thinking of his own life beyond Chapelon, her captain inwardly prayed that this dedicated young watch keeper would not remain a seafarer for too many years.

Then into this orderly workplace strolled a complete contrast. The chief engineer casually ambled into the wheelhouse from its rear door that led to the accommodation below. He briefly paused by the chart console, removing a battered pair of spectacles, largely held together with Araldite. He then carefully adjusted his glasses bridge, fashioned from an old piece of fuse wire that had for countless years replaced the original item when it broke, before putting them on again. His film star salary equalled the master's, but his thrifty, some would say miserly habits were legendary, known not only among his shipmates, but throughout the company too! Not that he was always miserly. His generosity on the rare occasions he went ashore with junior staff was almost bottomless. He casually shuffled up to his captain, briefly discussed why their departure was delayed, before telephoning his colleagues down in 'The Pit'. His self-imposed duties on the bridge ensured the engineers buried below his feet were kept advised with information they appreciated and could react to whenever the ship was on stand-by.

Within the ship's hierarchical divisions, the chief easily rivalled the master in status. This was shown by the four gold stripes on his epaulettes, had he ever bothered to wear them. Just like the tie that was supposed to be worn with his uniform. On other ships, the relationship between these great men could cause arguments and tensions. Not on Chapelon though. Despite their opposing personalities, both men were convivial with each other and managed their ship efficiently. The bridge team always warmly welcomed their chief engineer with his casual ways and his own specialist expertise. He automatically gravitated towards the senior cadet and the engine control desk to the right of the steering console, before rapidly scanning the annunciator lights, tapping the starting air pressure gauge and offering jovial words of encouragement. He was the ship's only confirmed bachelor of long standing and had no family ties or links with the land. He was probably the only individual on-board who was totally indifferent about whether Christmas was spent in Dunkirk, at sea or in Grangemouth. There was and remained a standing joke among the crew that spread way beyond Chapelon concerning his matrimonial bliss. It was said to emanate from the drawing boards of Sulzer Brothers in Switzerland, with the marine engine manufacturers of Burmeister and Wain in Denmark as an alternative mistress!

Built in the mid Nineteen Seventies and named in honour of France's greatest steam locomotive designer, Chapelon; a fifteen thousand tonnes deadweight multi-purpose cargo ship was now middle aged. At all times throughout her working life she had been carefully maintained to a high standard and apart from some necessary, but brutal and ugly fittings that were essential for her work, was very pleasing to the eye. Her versatile dry cargo ship design was already becoming obsolete in a world that opted for more specialist sea transport. That though did not stop her being ideal for the trading patterns she undertook among old French colonial ports scattered around the oceans of the world. At many of these, where wharfage was limited and often primitive, her design and flexibility were ideal. Her own comprehensive suite of cargo handling equipment and relatively compact size meant she could be worked efficiently in such places. For now, as she quietly sat part loaded, alongside in Dunkirk she was able to show off her graceful curves and the elegant flare of her bow to full effect.

From her forward, raised forecastle with its powerful anchor handling machinery, five holds stretched back to her accommodation and bridge front. Two of the four 'deep' tanks built into the bottom of number five hold had already been filled with heavy oil sludge cleaner, ready for unloading at Abidjan. Immediately behind number five hold, where the sides of the ship began to converge towards her stern was the engine room. Brightly lit with glistening cream paint, the curvature of the plating and framework did not spoil the impression of a cathedral like space that included an air conditioned and sound proof control room. This allowed the duty engineers to monitor their domain in relative comfort. In the heat and noise of the engine room proper, Chapelon's engineering staff had the necessary equipment and spares, including a powerful overhead crane and well-equipped workshop for carrying out their own complex maintenance and repairs. This same single space also provided all the services necessary for running the ship including electricity. Enough to power a small town. Dominating all though, like a brooding monster, towering past deck after deck was the ship's main engine. Capable of producing nearly seven thousand horse power from within its six massive cylinders, at a mere one hundred and ten RPM; the huge, low speed, two stroke, Sulzer diesel engine was coupled directly to the ship's single propeller, itself an impressive sculpture of magnesium bronze. Strapped to the huge engine's side were two bulky turbochargers that forced air into the Sulzer's cavernous cylinders, literally consuming the massive machine's own might and thunder.

Four decks were constructed around and behind the engine room casing above the ship's hull, mostly containing the ship's accommodation. This culminated with the navigation bridge on its top deck. Finally, behind the accommodation block was a smaller, refrigerated cargo hold.

Chapelon was without doubt an elegant ship, well cared for, competently crewed and pleasing to the eye.

It took only minutes before the squall blew itself clear. As the mooring parties extracted themselves from what shelter they had found on Chapelon's exposed decks, they started swearing at a light covering of snow that had now added to their discomfort and difficulties. The wind meanwhile remained a constant force, harsh and biting.

It was time to leave. Commands were spoken into hand-held radios. The chief engineer telephoned his colleagues down below, warning them of impending engine movements. The pilot spoke into the bridge VHF radio set, requesting the two tugs start pulling, while at the same time the remaining lines were let go fore and aft. The wheel was set 'hard to port', as the tugs started to gently ease the ship away from her berth. Leaning out over the stern, the second mate reported that the propeller was clear of obstructions for engine movements.

The seamen making up his after stand-by team were now visibly shivering and soaked with cold, filthy water as they worked the after winches, bringing their last link with the shore on-board. Coiling the polypropylene stern line on deck, the after crew were at least thankful that the steel back spring, which like all wire ropes possessed a bloody-mindedness of its own, self-stowed on a large winch drum.

"Dead slow ahead" was the order. Tightening his grip on the bridge control throttle lever, the senior cadet pushed it forward. From the funnel behind the bridge came a muted, hissing roar. In the engine room, air pressurised to twenty-one bars was blasted into the Sulzer's cavernous cylinders. Pistons were forced to move under this surge of energy and then continued their motion from expanding hot gasses as fuel was burned. The ship was under way and making way. As the engine caught, the senior cadet smoothly pulled the throttle back towards its upright position, setting eleven revolutions per minute on the RPM gauge, shouting confirmation that the engine was turning. Below his feet in the engine room, compressors were started, replenishing the vital air that had already been used. This would now be a constant worry for the engineers as the ship's working air reserves were depleted every time the Sulzer was stopped and re-started, a necessity when changing from ahead to astern, or vice-versa. When the bridge team took it upon themselves to sound off like spouting whales on the air operated whistle as well, the compressed air situation could become critical, even when every compressor was working flat-out. With them just starting their voyage, the control room instruments confirmed there was still plenty of air and everything was functioning properly and smoothly. That still didn't stop the third engineer and his junior grabbing a set of ear defenders each, before entering the noise and heat of the engine room, to conduct a close, visual inspection of their domain. The third engineer had also remained surprisingly tight lipped when his colleague asked about his wife and daughter who unbeknown to many of them were now settling into his en-suite cabin.

The ship's tall and slightly portly second engineer was dour and pessimistic by nature. He remained casually seated in the control room, sipping coffee and glowering at his own starting console and throttle lever as he idly swung in a well-used and slightly stained swivel chair. His personal thoughts silently and moodily reflected about the days when deck officers on the bridge, the likes of which he regarded as a sub species, only had a telegraph to play with had been bad enough. Now some idiot had decided to entrust them with controlling the engine directly. He had to grudgingly accept it but such logic he would never understand! Even the chief was up there with them, preening themselves in their uniforms, rather than joining his true colleagues in a boiler suit. The second's was casually unbuttoned down to his 'Y' Fronts, revealing an impressive appendix scar.

The dank, brackish water stirred with gentle reluctance around the ship's transom stern. There was barely a hint of vibration from the slowly revolving propeller and an engine that was turning at a seemingly impossibly low speed. The constant, biting wind was ever there though, presenting an immediate problem. Not only did Chapelon need to clear her berth, she also had to avoid another ship moored close ahead of her. Her bows were not swinging fast enough, while the tugs, struggling on full power fought to get her clear. Her part loaded hull and the bulk of her accommodation block were presenting themselves broadside to the near gale that was blowing. The wheel was quickly ordered back to amidships and half astern was called on the engine. The senior cadet now pulled the throttle to 'stop', briefly paused and pulled it back. Below, the precious air reserves moved cam shafts that set the exhaust valves for operating in reverse before blasting into the cylinders again. As he adjusted the engine speed to forty-two RPM, the senior cadet prepared to sound three short blasts on the whistle to signal their new movement. The chief engineer standing close by, briefly touched his arm and wagged a finger in a negative motion. Nobody had asked for it and there was no need to waste air! They both grinned at each other conspiratorially as the ship started to shudder and vibrate in response to its new command.

Chapelon cleared her neighbouring ship on the second attempt as the engine was once again set on dead slow ahead. Aided by the two tugs she gently negotiated the channels that formed the complexities of Dunkirk Eastern Port, her destination a lock that would grant access to the open sea. Out on deck, the frozen, muttering, mooring teams had to remain out in the open until the lock was cleared. Once the ship was inside the lock, they would have to then constantly tend her lines as the water level was adjusted.

They could not even make a start on storing their ropes and other paraphernalia in the forecastle locker and lazarette, a tiny diminutive hold, butting on to the ship's transom stern. It was a thankless task they were performing. Nobody could doubt that for now, they really were earning their seemingly generous keep.

In less than half an hour they arrived at the open lock gates, just in time for another snow flurry to sweep across the decks. Wind eddies now added to their ship handling problems, challenging the bridge's attempts to bring Chapelon smoothly alongside the lock's wall. It simply added to the irritation that was collectively being felt by her groaning, exposed mooring crews. Finally, heaving lines were thrown and ropes run ashore as the massive lock gates closed behind them. As they glowered in envy at the snug, enclosed bridge, none of the ship's mooring teams even had the time to seek brief shelter in warm messes and bring hot drinks out to their colleagues. The lock's water level was already falling, forcing them to work their lines carefully, as the wind maintained a constant threat. Some dejectedly puffed on difficult to light cigarettes, while all stamped their feet and flapped their arms in futile attempts to put warmth into their deep-chilled bodies.

After what seemed an eternity the lock gate ahead of the ship finally opened, exposing everybody to a fresh blast of icy, salt laden wind, coming straight in off a turbulent sea. Ropes, that were literally their final links with France were recovered by mariners who now functioned like robots. The tugs were already starting to lose interest in their charge as the

Sulzer alone started to gently power the ship with a new purpose. As soon as Chapelon had safely cleared the lock, the two small tugs released themselves with obscene haste and scuttled back into its protective shelter. Chapelon was now able to independently negotiate the widening channels of the western port as she headed for the entrance between massive breakwaters that guarded the entire complex of Dunkirk Harbour. With the biting wind, snow and increasing amounts of bitter, salt spray to contend with, there was no shortage of volunteers among the mooring crews for working in the holds to stow snaking ropes into coils. At long last they could finally tidy up forecastle and poop. The ship was carefully battening down for what was going to be a very rough voyage. Forward, exposed to everything the weather could throw at him, the mate tried to hide his misery and own dark thoughts. The ship was navigating confined waters without the aid of tugs. In an emergency, an anchor may be needed at short notice. He and a senior petty officer remained close to the windlass's controls, practically bereft of shelter. As they slid past a roll-on-roll-off passenger ferry busy at a link span, they let their minds drift to thoughts of imaginary debauchery going on in her cabins. For them, the fairer sex was about to be confined to sleazy magazines and the odd, dodgy film, hidden away in Chapelon's accommodation.

With her engine set on half-ahead, Chapelon safely cleared the breakwaters and was able to dig her bows into the open sea. The mooring crews meanwhile, managed to stow their gear and battened down hatches in record time. Without even glancing at the mate and his petty officer, maintaining their vigil at the windlass, departing colleagues beat a hasty retreat towards the accommodation and the thoughts of finally being able to partake of warmth and sustenance. Beneath their feet, the ship was already surging with movement as she met head on with short, steep seas, whose crests were being swept into white breaking masses by the wind. The spray that now periodically engulfed the forecastle stung the exposed skin of the mate and his colleague as they maintained their vigil at the windlass, tasting saltiness around their lips. Salt crystals even penetrated their layers of clothing, making them feel gritty and dirty within. Five minutes later, the ship slowed and was swung creating a lee on its port side.

The pilot could now disembark down a purpose-built rope ladder and into a waiting launch. For the two men maintaining their vigil on the windlass, it meant they could finally leave the most exposed part of the ship to her own devices, as around them the weather continued to noticeably deteriorate.

Leaning far out over the bridge wing side, the master watched carefully as the pilot safely boarded his launch that then immediately and rapidly swung away, cleaving through the waves towards the shelter of the breakwaters. For a brief moment Chapelon's captain felt a yearning to be with him, on his high-speed craft, as his thoughts turned to his own family and being denied yet another Christmas with them. He briefly watched as their first trip cadet and a seaman struggled to retrieve the specialist rope ladder the pilot had used, unlash it and stagger under its weight to stow it under cover.

With her engine stopped for disembarking the pilot and for the moment powerless, the ship was already performing bad-tempered, sluggish rolls as she lay to the mercy of wind and sea.

Briefly stumbling against Chapelon's motion, her master turned to the wheelhouse door and boldly ordered, "Full ahead." There was a pause, followed by the familiar roar of starting air as the Sulzer began to rumble. This time though, the massive engine was about to show its true muscle.

He allowed the third mate to take the con, guiding the ship through Dunkirk's approach fairway as they steamed towards the Eastbound Lane of the English Channel's traffic separation scheme. The visibility was reasonable and the master showed the briefest of smiles as he discreetly watched his most junior officer busy himself with navigating Chapelon. Being given the opportunity to take charge of the ship in confined waters had lifted any possible hint of the young man's own dark thoughts about leaving their native France and having Christmas in some godforsaken hole in Scotland. He was now clearly enjoying the professional challenge he had been given. The engine throttle was advanced forwards to set eighty-four RPM on the Sulzer; Chapelon's full manoeuvring speed, as the ship gently accelerated to eleven knots.

The wind now howled unabated, causing Chapelon to roll and pitch as her hull easily cleaved its way through a troubled sea; with its marching, white crested waves. The master and chief engineer meanwhile were deep in a muted conversation at the rear of the wheelhouse. Soon, once they were clear of the Dunkirk fairway, The master would call for, 'Full away on passage.' It would signal the formal commencement of their voyage to Grangemouth. The engineers would finally be able to take charge of the Sulzer working up its revolutions to full passage speed. Then, heavy fuel oil would be substituted for the clean, but expensive marine gas oil that was used for manoeuvring. HFO as it was more commonly known was dirty, near black and viscous. When heated, its viscosity would be sufficiently reduced to allow for its injection into the Sulzer's voluminous cylinders and provide energy for its motive power. At less than half the price of gas oil, its use on passage was absolutely essential if the ship was to make a profit. The chief engineer, ever worried about his engine, wanted to give the Sulzer a good blast, pushing settings a little above their normal one hundred and ten RPM, its nominal full, cruising speed. Their coastal voyages so far had seen several reduced speed demands where the HFO had not been switched over to gas oil. The chief was now fretting about exhaust carbon and unburnt fractions of the HFO depositing themselves on cylinder walls and in his engine's scavengers. He was also aware that the four hundred and fifty tonnes of HFO they had loaded in Dunkirk for their coming voyage to West Africa, was grottier and more sulphurous than usual. The master had contrasting demands to contemplate though. He had to balance the chief's mechanical concerns with his own worries about the deteriorating weather they would be facing as they beat their way up the North Sea towards Scotland. Theoretically, their part-laden draft would allow the ship to safely navigate inshore of recommended deep-water routes in the North Sea. He had already decided they would follow the offshore routes. They would keep Chapelon well clear of land, until they turned for the shelter of the Firth of Forth. With Easterly severe gales, he had no intention of getting too close to the coast and a lee shore! Also, this same severe weather would inevitably generate short, but steep waves, famed and notorious in the North Sea. Those had the potential to place undue stress and strain on his ship's hull, unless he maintained a sensible speed. On top of those problems there was also the visibility to consider. That too was a potential and unpredictable problem. To his credit, the ship's owner would never expect him to drive his ship recklessly. This still didn't negate the contrasting needs of Chapelon's two senior men. One had the sole interest of his surrogate child, the massive Sulzer, as his heartfelt worry. The other had to take a greater, more strategic view about his ship's overall wellbeing.

While their ship was being driven eastwards, directly into the weather and those notorious short, steep, seas they agreed to set the 'full away,' RPM at ninety-seven. That would equate with about thirteen knots. After leaving the channel separation scheme to the north west of The Scheldt, Chapelon would then be swung north into the deep-water routes that kept them safely away from the shore. The course change would now place the seas and weather on her starboard beam, easing stresses on the ship's hull. It was then that they would review their full away requirements again, hopefully allowing the chief to increase his engine's RPM. Then he could give his precious Sulzer the power blast he felt it deserved! Thus they had arrived at a true compromise. Neither man was entirely happy, but both felt they could support and justify what they had agreed.

Next on their agenda was the ever-demanding planned maintenance programme that Chapelon's owner uncompromisingly insisted upon. It was always subject to constant scrutiny and checking by the company's superintendents. One of the main engine's units, as each of the six-cylinder assemblies was known, was now due for a general overhaul.

To do that meant they would have to disable the ship's propulsion system for two days. Ignoring the plans and pleas from his engine room staff when they thought Chapelon would have Christmas in her own port, the chief had insisted the work would take place while the ship was safely alongside in Dunkirk. With the sudden change to their schedule, both senior men automatically agreed the work had to be done before the ship left Grangemouth; be it alongside, or in a sheltered anchorage in the Firth of Forth. The master promised the chief he would make sure the necessary requirements would be telegraphed ahead to their agent in Grangemouth. Ever fiercely patriotic and aware of real language difficulties when it came to using English on his ship, the master decided the message should be telegraphed via a French Coast Radio Station. Doing it that way would also spare the radio officer of having to struggle with what he perceived as being equally obdurate, Francophile, British Radio operators.

Immediate business done, the chief sauntered off down below, while the master remained on his bridge. He quietly chuckled as he settled into the tall chair provided for his exclusive use on the port-side of the wheelhouse, as he glanced at his departing senior colleague's footwear. The chief engineer was wearing an old pair of carpet slippers. He hardly ever bothered to change out of them, even when greeting the most senior of guests on board. The exception was when he needed to put on a pair of working boots that accompanied a boiler suit. Clothing he changed into whenever he entered the domain over which he had overall charge.

While his ship continued its passage up the buoyed fairway out of Dunkirk, the master was obliged to remain firmly on the bridge. Chapelon was now corkscrewing through the churning sea with salt spray constantly battering the wheelhouse windows and their groaning wipers. Close by, the sliding port wheelhouse door was wedged wide open offering instant access to the lee bridge wing. Regardless of how hot or frigid the weather might be, all of his deck officers insisted that an efficient lookout could not be maintained from a position that was remote from the outside environment. To emphasise the need for outside access and adding to their watch keeping problems, some of Chapelon's deck fittings – and in particular the substantial diverging masts of a Stulken heavy lift derrick presented numerous blind spots, hindering his watch keepers as they tried to constantly monitor the environment around them. The only way around this problem was to constantly move around the bridge. As captain, he thoroughly approved of their efforts and vigilance.

Old familiar sounds now started to enliven his senses. The gyro repeaters continued to click happily away to themselves, following the commands of their sensitive master instrument tucked away next to the chart table. The two radar sets were constant with their reassuring, high-pitched whine, while a muted chatter emerged from the VHF radio set. The third mate, ever efficient, busied himself with his duties. He was a likeable, reliable young man with a honed sense of responsibility. His similarly aged shore-side compatriots were probably still at university or completing other, higher education courses. Possibly only the armed services could offer such onerous responsibilities to people of a similar age – and no doubt they paid less too! Meanwhile, still keeping close to the engine control desk, the senior cadet maintained the movement book without supervision. His turn to wear a coveted gold stripe with a diamond on his sleeve, with its attendant film star pay packet would no doubt soon arrive.

The first trip cadet meanwhile had been sent out onto the weather bridge wing to take some visual bearings with an azimuth ring fitted, gyro compass repeater. The captain watched him noticeably stagger against the force of the wind and roll of the ship, gripping the repeater's pedestal as he stepped up to its slightly raised platform. Chapelon's Old Man smiled softly. They had all been through it at the start of their seafaring careers – and judging by the pallor of his face, the fresh air would do him good! He discreetly continued to observe his third mate as he quickly paid a visit behind the chart console, confirming their position and ensuring their Mark 21 Decca Navigator was properly aligned. The helmsman, without instruction, peered into a periscope in front of his steering console, calling out the standard compass heading, as he looked up into the binnacle on the monkey island, the deck space above the wheelhouse. Without the need of instruction, the senior cadet smoothly swapped the movement book for a piece of chalk, updating a blackboard that displayed the ship's heading and course information. As always, nothing aboard Chapelon was being left to chance. The ship was back at sea and in the element she was built for; a living, moving creature, driven by the pounding heartbeat of her engine. This transformation was already starting to positively affect all of her crew. The intensity of their disappointment about not seeing their loved ones over Christmas was almost magically being attenuated. With some reluctance the master turned his attention to a folder of paperwork he had brought with him. Essential work, but at times it felt onerous. Deep within, a part of him would have willingly swapped the wind-swept starboard bridge wing and gyro repeater with the first trip cadet, who was now crouched within the shelter of its dodger, throwing up into a scupper. The Old Man's first priority was to quickly pen a message about the planned unit overhaul onto a blank radio telegram form before asking for it to be taken to the radio office. Next he reviewed the various notes of protest he had submitted in Dunkirk. These were mostly about cargo, its condition and delays. There had also been other problems that had affected the revenue earning capacity of his ship too. He worked rapidly through the details with an experienced eye, cross-checking his work with a bundle of bills-of-lading and their confirming documentation that added to the bulk to his file. As the ship's owner, lawyers, insurers and shippers argued their cases, no doubt there would be more questions to answer in future. For now, everything appeared to be orderly and justified ready for their arrival at Grangemouth. He now started scanning a recently completed cargo manifest, matching the new bills-of-lading with recently loaded cargo. This included over three hundred tonnes of classified dangerous goods, better known in the trade as blue book cargo. Included were pesticides, herbicides and lead based anti-knock additives for petrol. Even these hazardous substances did not overly worry him. They were pretty standard for the ship's usual trading routes. His next self-appointed task was to check the completed loading plan for Grangemouth, an untimely reminder of the unexpected and not particularly welcome arrival of the ship's agent, only oh so recently in Dunkirk. Over three thousand tonnes all told, including a significant amount in containers. He quickly noted that part of the Grangemouth consignment was one hundred and fifty tonnes of commercial gelignite, fuses and blasting caps. For Chapelon and her versatility, just another routine cargo. It would be safely tucked away into purpose-built magazine lockers down in number two lower hold. Purely based on the cargo they were so far carrying and the consignments they were also expecting, along with the ports they would be calling at, the voyage to West Africa looked boringly unspectacular.

It was the high value cargo that commanded premium freight rates – and had also wrecked their Christmas plans that briefly played on his curiosity though. For a few moments his imagination ran wild as he wondered why on earth consignees in Abidjan and Monrovia needed thirty-thousand, state-of-the-art Swedish cash registers.

The third mate calling for his attention gave Chapelon's captain a legitimate excuse to abandon his paperwork. He instinctively eased himself out of his high chair and immediately became aware of the increase in surging movement of his ship that he now felt through his feet. At that same moment, the second mate strode into the wheelhouse, features still raw and pinched from his 'standby' in filthy weather at the stern. This officer was in his early thirties, stocky and of medium height. With a pencil line moustache, he always looked dapper regardless of the circumstances he faced. He was highly competent at his job, but also appeared aloof and slightly distant from his colleagues, even showing discreet signs of resentment about having his commander on the bridge with him. A native of Provence he had distinctly olive skin and matching deep brown, searching eyes.

Beyond the spray splattered wheelhouse windows the ship was now approaching the fairway buoy that marked the entrance to Dunkirk's channel and the third mate was absolutely correct to let his captain know. Grabbing a pair of binoculars, the master joined his junior colleagues where their bodies absorbed the movement of the ship as they stood together immediately behind the wheelhouse windows, deep in conversation. Soon, he could order, 'full away,' to be rung on the engine and their passage proper would commence. Having finished their brief conference, the two junior officers decided they wanted to flog the clocks, putting ship's time back an hour to GMT during the night watches. The master's approval was almost a formality. Each of the three bridge watches would work an extra twenty minutes during the night, so that clocks could be aligned with time kept in their destination port. He briefly nodded his assent as he scanned the forward horizon with his seven by fifties. The wind was now blowing a full gale and the ship was getting noticeably lively. To the north of them, an isolated snow squall formed a smudge against a dull, morose and yellow horizon that tried to push itself from beneath the overcast.

Otherwise, the troubled, murky waters of the channel reflected a grey sky. Despite spume being swept off breaking wave tops, visibility at least remained acceptable. Shipping traffic meanwhile was heavy but then it always was in the eastern channel. One blessing was there were no reports by coastguards of rogue vessels travelling the wrong way up the eastbound lane of the traffic separation scheme they were about to enter.

The third officer quietly waited for his commander to complete his assessment of the traffic situation before confirming he had handed the bridge over to his more senior and newly arrived colleague. He asked whether he could leave the bridge. There was no real need to ask, but the master appreciated his manners and courtesy. He nodded with a smile, offering a warm and genuine thanks to the young man, who in contrast with his now brooding watch mate was open and honest about everything. As an afterthought, the master also suggested he might like to take the wretched first trip cadet with him!

Barely ten minutes later, 'full away' was rung on the control for the main engine.

Operation of the Sulzer was passed from the bridge to Chapelon's engineers working below their feet. It was they who made the switch to heavy fuel oil and gently began to ease the engine's revolutions up to the previously agreed passage speed. Shortly after, Chapelon swung into the eastbound lane of the traffic separation scheme and started butting directly into the weather. Water now spurted from her hawse pipes within which her stockless anchors were secured. At the same time, massive sheets of spray rose over her bows as she thudded into incoming waves. Her passage into deteriorating weather had now well and truly begun. The master remained on the bridge long enough to be satisfied that his ship was not being pushed too hard, before retiring to his suite, one deck below. This allowed the second mate to take full charge of the ship as he prowled his domain like a brooding, stalking cat.

Unlike lunch which had been a scrappy and hurried affair in the wake of their orders to sail, the master still felt contented from a formal but relaxed dinner in the dining saloon when he returned to a darkened bridge at twenty-one hundred hours. His honed, seaman senses instinctively told him it was obvious that the weather had deteriorated still further and the gale had intensified in its severity. He was at least pleased that the third mate who always greeted him with gusto was back on duty, standing his night watch.

Blackout curtains drawn across the front and sides of the chart console now constantly moved with the ship's motion as she pitched and slammed into seas that had mounted in ferocity. A pair of angle poise lamps above the chart table had been dimmed to an orange glow allowing barely sufficient light to read the chart beneath them. To stop it rolling off the chart, a pencil was sandwiched in the middle of a pair of parallel rulers. As Chapelon bucked and heaved beneath his feet, everything creaked in unison from the bridge fittings to the massive steel frames that held his ship together. The master wedged himself against the chart table as he read the latest weather forecast. It was far from encouraging. Even the shrieking and howling wind around the ship's superstructure failed to mask the roar and crash of breaking seas as they slammed into Chapelon's hull and played in her curling wake.

A friendly shouted greeting coming from the near pitch-black wheelhouse front confirmed the location of his third officer. This was immediately followed by information about some freshly brewed coffee. After part filling a mug, the master cautiously made his way towards his duty watch keeper letting his eyes slowly accustom themselves to the darkness around him. He found his young officer busily monitoring their visibility as he assessed the loom that was showing around their foremast navigation light and automatically checked distances of visible ships on a conveniently close-by radar set. The third mate finally announced it was barely more than three miles. Acceptable for safety without impinging on their passage routine, but only just. The other radar had been cranked out to a longer range, with the Oosterschelde clearly visible on its screen. Soon they would turn north bound for the recommended deep-water routes used by traffic transiting the east coast of the United Kingdom. This was why the master had returned to the bridge. Such a course alteration was normally well within the capabilities of his officers without his presence or supervision. It was the severity of the weather that meant he wanted to be there on *his* bridge. The chief engineer's unannounced arrival in the wheelhouse came as no surprise either as he ambled around to join his colleagues, a steaming mug already in his hand. There was no need to tell the chief where the coffee was. His sense of smell had already deduced that, as with his singular sense of purpose he immediately and decisively studied the dimly lit engine RPM gauge.

For now, the third mate deliberately ignored the muttered conversation between Chapelon's two great men as he prepared to swing the ship north onto her new heading. The previously unseen duty quartermaster quietly emerged from the shadows when he was asked to close the starboard wheelhouse door and open the port one in readiness for taking weather on their starboard beam. The young deck officer meanwhile concentrated on the radar set that had been cranked out to long-range. Skilfully his hands worked the variable range ring and bearing marker, while at the same time he glanced up at the depth readings being displayed on their Simrad Echo Sounder, mounted high on the wheelhouse's front bulkhead. Moving rapidly and easily, absorbing the pitch and roll of the ship, he disappeared behind the chart console to confirm their position on the chart, cross checking his range, bearing and depth soundings with the Mark 21 Decca Navigator. They had a mile to run to their alter course position. Before departing from the chart table, the third mate thoughtfully disabled their off-course alarm. A device in its own little rosewood box that contained a magnetic compass whose card had a strip of foil running along its length. Should a light shining above fail to reflect on the foil, then an alarm was sounded, indicating a problem with the ship's steering; or a blown bulb. Pleasurably, the master discreetly observed his officer with quiet satisfaction. The ship's navigation, bridge and traffic management were all being kept under competent control.

With the quartermaster ready to take charge of the helm, the Old Man did raise an eyebrow when his watch keeping officer moved across to the Arkus autopilot / steering console. Engaging manual helm, he started to steer the ship himself, glancing over at the radar before making his port turn that put Chapelon on her new heading. That was certainly not textbook bridge management! However, in the faint, muted glow of light emerging from the gyro repeater compass card he discerned the look of contentment on his most junior officer's face as he practiced his steering skills with Chapelon. The master let the minor transgression pass without comment. That his third mate was maintaining such skills was beneficial in its own right – and he was handling the ship superbly, despite the appalling weather, applying timely counter helm to effortlessly steady the ship on her new course, before reengaging the autopilot.

Chapelon's motion suddenly and dramatically changed. The starboard wheelhouse door now rattled constantly in response to being exposed to the full fury of the elements.

Her previous pitching and slamming virtually disappeared to be replaced by pronounced and heavy rolling. In the darkness of the bridge, coffee mugs and spoons crashed onto the deck while the litter bin went its own way, liberally freeing itself of its contents. The creaking of frames and fittings became more monotonous and regular as everybody straddled their legs and reached for hand holds. On the accommodation decks below, anything not properly secured including a number of private radio sets in the crews' cabins crashed and grated while those with weak stomachs groaned at the latest assault on their digestion. The third mate and his quartermaster cautiously ventured out onto the port bridge wing to check exposed decks using their powerful and portable signal lamp as a searchlight. In its narrow, penetrating beam, dense clouds of spray lashed across the starboard side, but it was only that, spray. Not green seas that could have really brought about chaos and damage. The carefully secured decks presented a marked contrast with the falling books and nose-diving hi-fi systems in the cabins and spaces below. At least for now, the main decks remained safe and seaworthy. Five minutes later, content that the ship was settled on her new heading and was avoiding conflicting traffic, the third officer shrugged himself out of an anorak he had hastily donned before leaving the shelter of the wheelhouse and joined the ship's great men; but not before remembering to reset the off-course alarm.

To those unfamiliar with the niceties of ships encountering extreme seas, Chapelon, as she now rolled heavily into the steep waves, whilst taking a beating on her starboard side, may have found the experience terrifying. In reality the stress on the ship's structure had been considerably reduced. She was riding the seas far more comfortably now she was no longer slamming headlong into the weather. The chief engineer's response to the new feel of their ship was immediate. He boldly announced he wanted to increase main engine revolutions. The master, having given the problem the briefest of final thoughts, reluctantly agreed. There was no technical reason why they should not proceed with the chief's proposal, but the captain's instincts about the manoeuvre still put a feeling of unease in his stomach. He then made a sudden and unexpected provisory. The engine room would remain manned during the hours of darkness. A seamanlike precaution that also helped mitigate his own worries and concerns about deteriorating weather and visibility.

The chief engineer's response was to sharply draw at his breath and then swear at his colleague. The third officer was able to diplomatically hide his feelings of relief following his captain's new instructions. There would be no review of this command until daylight and it was quite clear that the ship's commander was in no mood to negotiate.

While the engine's throttle was gently eased further open by the chief's compatriots below, the chief engineer decided to go and discuss this latest bombshell with his engineering team face-to-face. The ship's crewing levels assumed that the engine room would be routinely unmanned outside working hours whenever the ship was settled on passage.

Thinking of his second engineer in particular, the chief visibly winced as he pictured the torrent of abuse that was about to be directed straight at him!

Chapter 2

The Weather Picture

"A mid-latitude depression in the North Atlantic Ocean will release the same energy as an atomic bomb being detonated every fifteen minutes." The meteorology lecturer was graphically impressing new students about the forces at work in the planetary weather systems. "Now if I were a dollop of wind..." he continued, projecting his paunch and striding around his lectern.

To the untrained eye, meteorological charts often fail to portray that weather is dynamic, physical and most important of all, three dimensional.

In an era when understanding the jet stream and its driving forces was in its infancy, the weather as understood by most, was generated beneath the tropopause, a permanent temperature inversion, tens of thousands of feet above the ground. The Trop as it is commonly referred to also acts as a lid on what is colloquially known as the lower atmosphere. Above it is the almost sterile and near uniform stratosphere.

As Chapelon continued her passage north towards Grangemouth, meteorologists across Europe were extremely busy. At Bracknell in Berkshire, housed in a large, plain and seemingly soulless monolithic building was the United

Kingdom Meteorological Office. Here, forecasters and their support staff were tasked with making sense of the complexities they faced with their ever-changing mid-latitude weather. To help them resolve their problems they had computing power that for the time was unique in the United Kingdom. Essential for maintaining its work, the Meteorological Office also housed a complex global communications hub that processed and distributed information around the clock. Constant streams of weather observations from satellites, aircraft, ships at sea and regional weather centres were its lifeblood. In addition to their own observations the regional centres collected and collated information from a network of volunteer auxiliary observers who diligently submitted reports from every point in the United Kingdom. Their ranks included air traffic controllers, harbour masters, coastguards, colleges, schools and a plethora of other public-spirited individuals whose common interest was the weather. Their collective observations helped to populate gaping holes that would have otherwise appeared in the weather puzzle, vastly improving the accuracy of forecasters' predictions. Amid this, round-the-clock hive of activity charts were constantly updated with symbols that were – and remain internationally agreed. Our charismatic meteorology lecturer blatantly and frequently reminded his classes that the world only had two truly universal languages; music and met!

Largely misunderstood and often ignored by the general public, weather forecasters are at times regarded as some of the most derided professionals in the world. Aviators and mariners at least, appreciate their skills and understand the enormous difficulties they face. Even with state-of-the-art computing power and fed with frequent and reliable observations, there will be times when it becomes nigh-on-impossible to accurately predict the movement and causative effects of air masses, cyclones, fronts and anticyclones.

Short comings apart, their work remains essential when it comes to the safe passage of ships and aircraft and for the conduct of many other activities.

For the duty staff at Bracknell the inevitable annual debate about a possible white Christmas was an unwanted nuisance diversion, as they grappled with a complex and constantly changing puzzle. Powerful and conflicting weather systems were pushing and straining throughout the north eastern Atlantic Ocean affecting first the United Kingdom and then further into Western Europe. Extensive gale and severe gale warnings were already in force. On board the Chapelon, those predictions were all too apparent. Her master's decisions concerning plenty of sea-room and maintaining the engine on enhanced readiness had now been fully vindicated.

A deep depression also known as a cyclone lying off south east Iceland was not an unusual feature for the time of year. Expanding towards the south from the depression's centre, its leading warm front, pursued by a faster cold front had already started to merge or 'occlude'.

Unusually for winter though an area of high pressure – an anti-cyclone had anchored itself over Finland. From this feature was now extending a ridge of high pressure that pointed westwards across Norway. This effectively blocked the eastwards movement of the Icelandic depression. Hindered by this barrier, the depression started to intensify or deepen – and its winds accordingly rose in ferocity. The rotation of the earth further amplified these winds, forcing them to circulate in an anti-clockwise direction as they tried to neutralise the low pressure at the depression's centre.

A new anti-cyclone was also developing over Strasbourg, pushing its fringes out to the coast of Western Europe. Yet another Easterly moving Atlantic depression, that would have otherwise harried the Mediterranean and Southern Europe, now found itself being diverted north by this new feature, forcing it to swing across Ushant and disrupt the English Channel. Pummelled by the effects of the Strasbourg anticyclone, the depression's core started to change from being circular to sausage-like, before becoming near quasi-stationary in an area that encompassed and included the Cherbourg Peninsula.

Pooling their experience and aided by their computers, meteorologists had already made what they thought were sound and prognostic judgements...

In Nineteen Twenty-One, the Japanese Meteorologist Doctor Sakurei Fujiwhara made a discovery that rightly bears his name 'The Fujiwhara Effect'. Descriptively it is known as 'The Dumbbell Effect.' Doctor Fujiwhara was researching the impacts of tropical revolving storms. Typhoons, as they are commonly referred to in his part of the pacific are both intense and devastating.

It would take over forty years and the emergence of satellite technology before the brilliance of Doctor Fujiwhara's ground-breaking work was fully vindicated.

Noting how tropical storms could sometimes vastly exceed predictions about their ferocity, Doctor Fujiwhara decided to investigate what happens when two storms are drawn together. Sometimes they would merge; a recognised feature of depressions, not only in the tropics but in mid-latitudes too. At other times, the two centres of depression would start to rotate around each other, clockwise in the southern hemisphere, anti-clockwise in the north, taking on the form of a spinning dumbbell. Already ferocious weather then became decidedly worse. There were further scenarios and models for Doctor Fujiwhara to consider. What happens when two depressions of significantly different intensities fail to merge? He deduced that the smaller of the two depressions could be captured by and then rotate around the larger; gaining strength and impetus as it does. During the season when tropical revolving storms mature, this effect is both lethal and unpredictable. For those fortunate to live in – and also ply the oceans in mid-latitudes such intense devastation is fortunately extremely rare. Even when Fujiwhara's effect begins to develop, it is usually short-lived and far less dramatic then when it occurs in the tropics. Cooler climes, particularly sea temperatures encourage slower, more predictable energy movements. Also, in higher latitudes, merging air masses and their associated frontal systems help to nullify the malignant intensities of fully developed tropical revolving storms.

Unfortunately, the weather influencing the English Channel and North Sea that Christmas Eve was about to radically change from anything resembling normal.

The sausage shaped depression in the western channel split forming two new cyclones. This was undetected for several hours by meteorological services. The smaller of the two depressions, now centred between Cherbourg and Ushant started to orbit the larger; mirroring Doctor Fujiwhara's original predictions. Except that it was now further distorted by the high-pressure system whose heart was anchored over

Strasbourg. This complex development of depressions, previously quasi-stationary started to bodily move again, heading north-east through The English Channel, all the time being influenced by blocking and squeezing from the southern anti-cyclone.

Atrocious weather harried the Straits of Dover.

Gaining in intensity the anti-clockwise rotating, smaller depression then swung into the North Sea towards Jutland. Like a sled on rails, its larger brother began following the track of the occluding front from the Icelandic depression, tracking the east coast of England.

It was then that the ridge of high pressure from the anti-cyclone over Finland came into play, inhibiting further movement. The larger centre of the divided depression stalled in the North Sea, east of Norfolk. The smaller depression, circling its larger brother, was blocked and further compressed when it lay well to the west of Denmark. Finally, with the two depression centres mimicking spinning gear wheels, their intense fringes interacted with unrestrained fury, one hundred and fifty miles off the Cleveland / North Yorkshire coast, throwing off a massively ferocious easterly airstream. Limited in extent, but deadly.

The north east of England and Scottish Borders were about to endure the worst storm in living memory.

Chapter 3
The Night Watch

"Some night!" came the shouted greeting from the entrance to Tynemouth Castle as two men clad in heavy weather gear fought a shrieking wind and driving rain while they struggled with a pair of massive, ancient, oak gates; each heavily studded with wrought iron.

A slamming gale, streaming in from the near-by North Sea howled straight into an ancient, once fortified barbican behind the gates, where its fury now pounded against the huge, hinged barriers with sustained, physical force. The men who were valiantly trying to battle with the rawness of the elements were both in their mid-thirties, of medium height and build, one clean shaven, the other bearded. Their coastguard issue, black 'Weather Guard' jackets zipped up tight to their collars managed to keep their upper bodies dry as they strained against the first of their reluctant obstacles. The gates had originally been installed as part of the old castle's defences when the priory that had first occupied the site had seen the need to protect itself against those wishing it harm. It had been subject to siege and invasion over a tumultuous few centuries going back to the Dark Ages. And they worked! The old barriers remained formidable even against the modern-day users who were trying to gain a legitimate entry. Muscles cracking, they used all their strength as they finally managed to push one heavy piece of carpentry until it was nearly flush with the old, stained stonework of the barbican wall against which it was hinged before grasping a huge wrought iron hook and dropping it into its lug on the offered barrier.

Reeling against the storm and driving rain that now howled unrestrained through the barbican and threatened to knock them off their feet, they staggered over to the second gate for support and then repeated the process. The headlights of their cars, pulled over perilously close to a dry moat that plunged away from the castle's approach road illuminated little more than sheets of precipitation as they completed their strenuous and difficult task.

Carefully groping past The Turk's Head and White Horse; pubs that marked the seaward end of Tynemouth Village, another set of headlights swung onto the approach road and gently drove towards the barbican, drawing level with the two men, just as they finally secured the second gate. The driver wound down his window and issued a cheery greeting. In his early sixties, clean shaven, wizened and grinning broadly he finally called, 'Well done, lads!' in a broad Northumbrian accent, before continuing his warm and dry journey, through the barbican and into the castle grounds beyond. The two drenched men looked at each other; shrugged and chuckled. Although they rarely admitted it, both were extremely fond of their senior watch officer.

"Let's leave them open and get the day watch to do the same, otherwise we'll never get out of here in the morning," called Jack, the bearded coastguard as they returned to the warmth and dry of their own cars.

"Aye," agreed Roy his companion, "I don't think English Heritage need overly worry about mischief making youths on a night like this!"

Uncomfortably wet and battered, with the taste of salt spray as well as rain on their mouths, both gratefully sought the refuge of their elderly vehicles to continue a familiar commute that led through the generous grounds of Tynemouth Castle that lay beyond the gates.

Thoughtfully positioned sodium floodlights illuminated key parts of the old priory ruins around which the castle was protectively built. They highlighted structures and ramparts with their distinct orange glow as they stood sentinel against the elements that seemed bent on destruction. It had been thus for nearly a millennium. To the drivers' left, across a grassed space, the walls and ramparts could only be vaguely discerned through torrents of rain as they interrupted the even vaguer line of lights from the nearby coastal road and the Village of Cullercoats. Ahead of them, for the moment little more than a silhouette, was the outline of a modern building, cheerfully illuminated in some of its windows. A tall radio mast thrust its way into the darkened, troubled sky on one side of the structure whose architecture was supposed to sympathise with the historic site in which it sat. Short of and opposite the entrance of this new building and to their right, the main bulk of the old priory ruins terminated in a small, squat, roofed chapel; complete with period-stained glass windows. The Percy Chantry as it was known, had its own long and venerable history and remained a consecrated place of worship. Despite the supposed efforts of more modern architects, The Percy Chantry undoubtedly contrasted starkly with the building on their left which was barely five years old and built of yellow, sandy coloured blocks. On the new building's facing wall there was also a proud sign proclaiming, 'HM Coastguard, Tyne-Tees Maritime Rescue Sub-Centre'. For all of the rescue centre's modernity, even the site on which it stood had its own history. Coastguards in their various guises had been in occupation for over one hundred and sixty years, dating back to the organisation's origins in Eighteen Hundred and Twenty-Two, when it was desperately needed as an anti-smuggling force.

The little convoy of two vehicles swung sharply into a covered and illuminated car park whose roof formed the floor of emergency planning and operations rooms above their heads. To seawards, some protection was offered by steep reinforced earthworks that had once housed a modern, coastal defence battery of artillery, guarding the entrance of the near-by River Tyne. Snug against these earthworks were portacabins, the domain of English Heritage craftsman who during working days cared for and gently tended the old, historic site. A pair of rats, suddenly startled by the new arrivals, scurried across the carpark for cover. Solid, basement walls inset with brown doors that led to store rooms and an emergency generator room enclosed the rest of the space, where mid-way a set of steps led up to a glazed door. Affectionately christened 'The Tradesmen's Entrance', it was inevitably used for access by all of the station's regular staff.

The two men parked their elderly, down-trodden looking vehicles and walked together companionably. Despite the sheltered location, wind, rain and sea spray from the fury of the storm managed to still batter the seemingly snug car park.

The cars belonging to the watch they were relieving were now thickly caked in salt from the seas crashing on cliffs below them. They noted their senior watch officer's car, equally battered and decrepit, had already been vacated as he sought the warmth of the modern building. With low pay a current major issue, one of the station's management team had been heard to remark that the assessors tasked with investigating remuneration ought to plan a visit when this particular watch was on duty; dryly adding that the car park looked akin to a scrap-yard!

As they finally stepped inside and closed the door against the raging storm, they were grateful the rescue centre was warm, friendly, bright and welcoming. Broad stairs with gleaming stainless-steel rails swept up through the building. Many of the block work walls around the stairwell had been left exposed. Their grim and functional form seemed to suit the airiness of the modern design. Meanwhile, both men immediately headed for a small and well-equipped galley beyond which was a cosy and suitably appointed rest room.

Hanging up their dripping coats they quickly added food and beverage stocks to their watch's cupboard and with their briefcases made for the operations room. Their navy-blue woolly pullies, bereft of rank insignia, white shirts and black ties, identified them as coastguard watch officers. First, they passed through the emergency planning room with its airy, high, vaulted ceilings, whose otherwise austere centre was dominated by a large chart press. All the room's lights were extinguished, as sufficient illumination shone through a glazed partition ahead of them, leading to the operations room. As they entered the operations room proper through a heavy door, its fluorescent brilliance was a complete contrast to the subdued atmosphere they had left. The immediate impression was that of sterile nakedness. Cheerful exchanges and greetings were made with the watch that was about to depart as seats were swapped on specialist consoles that flanked the senior watch officer's own work station.

"What kept you, lads?" chuckled their boss, having nearly completed his own handover with his departing shift supervising colleague.

"Please note he is dry!" quipped Jack the bearded watch officer, gesticulating and grinning. Instantly becoming serious, he added, "We left the gates open. Best if you do the same, otherwise we'll be stuck."

His Yorkshire accent although not particularly broad, was noticeable. The two watch officers they were relieving spoke in the same dialect.

The departing senior watch officer's voice, by way of contrast showed no sign of regional preference or accent. Despite the atrocious weather, whose presence was apparent even in the snug, airy and safe operations room, the hand-over between watches was straight forward and routine. There were no incidents open, but constant referrals were made to a huge state board that faced them all. The meteorological conditions were the one subject of careful discussion and analysis. Both sets of watch officers carefully studied and debated the readings from an anemometer. Its display was placed high on the right-hand side of the operations room and directly in front of them.

"There's also a heavy swell coming through the breakwaters here," remarked one of the departing watch keepers as he stood leaning by the open operations room door and gesticulated across towards the River Tyne entrance. "Tynemouth Lifeboat has moved up river to Jarrow already."

That was a fairly routine precaution. The Arun Class Lifeboat, whose usual location was a fixed mooring, just down-river from the notorious Black Middens had now sought calmer waters, well clear of the Tyne's sea defences. Otherwise the lifeboat may have been damaged by the waves crashing through the river's entrance and over its breakwaters. It also meant that should the boat be needed there would be an inevitable delay in getting her out to sea. As well as the longer river transit her crew would need extra time to assemble at Jarrow on the Tyne's South side, rather than in Tynemouth, almost immediately below their coastguard station.

"Oh, and the rescue Helo at Boulmer is on her Christmas routine, so let The Air Rescue Co-ordination Centre know in good time, should you think you need her too. It's all there," he finally added, waving at the state board. "I'll be off then and happy Christmas."

His own watch had just completed a full round of duties and were looking forward to rest days over the festive period. By contrast, the new arrivals had just started. It was bang-on seven o'clock or nineteen hundred hours, the official change-over time. A large digital clock with red figures, centrally placed in front of them said so. During the winter months at least, local time and Greenwich Mean Time were the same.

The wizened senior watch officer, slight of build and with his thinning hair showing virtually no signs of grey scanned his RDCE, the abbreviation for his Radio Distribution and Control Equipment desk, fussily adjusting some of the switches that commanded several radio sites between the

Scottish Border and Robin Hood's Bay in North Yorkshire. He checked printed information on sheets beneath clear Perspex panels on the flat part of his console and cross checked them with the massive state-board that dominated the operations room in front of them. Once satisfied all was in order, he reached down for a very impressive sandwich box and carefully stowed it in a filing cabinet next to him. He was more than happy to let his two colleagues smoothly go through a series of checks on the equipment they controlled.

"Don't you two lads forget to fill-in your public holiday overtime," he fussed in a fatherly fashion, digging out his own overtime form.

They both smiled, as they made ready to do their radio checks. Jack had gone to the console on his left; the distress watch desk. This desk was larger than the others, with a modular extension on its right, housing controls and a display for VHF radio direction finding equipment. Immediately above the flat part of his desk were blue painted, angled panels that housed controls and light displays for all the VHF Radio sites in the district. These displays and controls were common to all the desks. A module mounted above those and unique to his desk was the 'Big Set'. The control unit for a SKANTI Medium Frequency radio transceiver. Out of habit Jack had already clad himself in a headset and boom microphone as he went to work.

"Forth Coastguard, Tyne Tees Coastguard, Radio Check Channel Sixteen."

He had selected the radio site at Newton in Rural Northumberland, whose village was birthplace to Jim, their senior watch officer. He wrote in the CG19; the official designation for the VHF Channel Sixteen log book as he spoke, operating the radio transmitter with a foot switch.

"Tyne, Forth, you are loud and clear." The Scottish Burr had a jaunty ring to it.

"Evening Forth, you too, Tyne out."

The radio procedure was abridged and slightly casual, appropriate for watches that knew each other well. All the time, his eyes scanned the orange 'busy' lights of his other radio sites as he simultaneously wrote in his log. He next keyed the Hauxley transmitter further up the coast from their building and blew into his microphone, checking receiver busy lights and the bearing on the radio direction finder mounted on their local mast. Working down past The Tyne, he finally tested their Whitby site.

"Humber Coastguard, Tyne-Tees Coastguard, Radio Check, Channel Sixteen."

"Tyne, Humber; evening, you're loud and clear."

It somehow seemed strange to hear a Scouse accent in Yorkshire!

"Humber, Tyne, you too, out." Jack immediately turned to the SKANTI, where he adjusted the set to go through an automatic self-checking routine, before calling near-by Cullercoats Coast Radio Station on 2182Khz, the set's Radiotelephony distress and calling frequency.

Roy, his colleague, sat to the right of their senior watch officer was also busy manipulating buttons, checking channel zero, a VHF radio frequency that had effectively metamorphosed into a private broadcasting net for the conduct of search and rescue and for handling routine traffic between specialist units. Then Roy turned his attention to their telephone lines. These too were copied identically on all the consoles. He immediately started checking a number of private telephone circuits linked to the Air Rescue Co-ordination Centre at Pitreavie near Edinburgh and with police control rooms in their district. Finally, he turned his attention to the private telephone circuit they had with Cullercoats Radio on nearby Marconi Point, across the bay to their North. A brief conversation about the weather and traffic ensued, before he disconnected the call.

"All checks complete," he announced to Jim, his senior officer who had charge of the Station Log, "subject to the base-set and pager."

"OK, Son, thanks for the reminder," responded their boss, as he took his attention away from a packet of cigarettes and checked the two specialist units mounted on his console.

The radio base set was self-contained and independent of the main radio systems in their district. It was an emergency back-up. The Motorola paging unit, his other specialist item could send coded tones across Channel Zero alerting coastguard teams and lifeboat crews. Jim made an appropriate note in his station log before striking a match and puffing away in contentment. The high ceilings meant the drifting fumes didn't bother his non-smoking colleagues. They were both relieved and grateful to note his obvious happiness though. They harboured raw, recent memories of when Jim had decided to give up smoking. Six weeks of sheer hell and tetchiness against Jack and Roy had followed before equilibrium was restored through nicotine.

Jim now rummaged through his brief case and produced that morning's copy of the Newcastle Journal. Ignoring the rest of the newspaper he sought out the crossword puzzle and reached for a pen.

A few minutes later, looking up from his task, he stretched in contentment and said, “Here’s a difficult one, lads, three letters; a refreshing drink, begins with T.”

“Nothing like a subtle hint,” responded Roy, still sat to his right, as he moved back from his desk. “You want a wet then, Jim? Coffee, Jack?” he asked his headphone clad colleague on the distress watch desk, who nodded.

“Yer a good lad, Roy,” chuckled Jim in alert anticipation as he searched through his huge sandwich box, producing a doorstop of a sandwich, a home-made scone and a chocolate snow ball.

Roy, the designated ‘wet’ maker grabbed a near-by tray and exited towards the galley.

Waiting for the kettle to boil, Roy wandered out of the galley and into the darkened rest room. He gazed through a rain spattered window towards the castle grounds and the floodlit ruins. Aware of the shrieking wind, even from inside the building, he thought of the domestic scene he had left behind, before coming on watch. His two young boys, bursting with excitement had scoured the house up and down for their presents and were already starting to test the patience of his wife. They had wisely decided to leave the main gifts hidden in the loft until he got home in the morning. Stocking fillers would have to satisfy the lads’ inevitable early rising that would herald the dawn of Christmas day. After the initial celebrations and salutations, he would need to sleep before his second night watch. Roy didn’t mind. The overtime was extremely useful and he was fond of the coastguard station, its location and his two colleagues. The pay was awful, but search and rescue was a worthwhile profession. The click of the boiling kettle returned his thoughts to his more immediate task.

Less than five minutes later he was back in the operations room, tray in hand. “People can die of thirst, you know,” remarked Jim, wiping scone crumbs from his mouth. Grinning, the designated ‘wet’ maker also gave his headset clad colleague on the distress watch desk a mug before returning to his own console, hot drink in hand.

Having finished his evening snack, Jim put his newspaper to one side and sipped his tea happily. Rummaging in his pocket he produced his handkerchief that he then carefully placed on his desk. He then delicately removed his false teeth and neatly placed them on top, ensuring they were in rapid reach before he almost seemed to fold himself comfortably into his chair, briefly closing his eyes in thought.

A ferocious and heavy gust of wind slammed into the substantial building producing a gentle shudder. Roy, instinctively and suddenly looked up at the Anemometer as his other colleagues too became alert to the new threat.

“Jeepers, that gust hit over eighty knots!” he proclaimed.

“Forecast is maximum of fifty-five,” remarked Jim, his boss. “I’ll have a chat with Port of Tyne Authority.”

“Ready for the inshore forecast broadcast?” asked Jack, ever mindful of his channel sixteen duties, as they spoke across their boss who was busy telephoning the port controllers further up the river.

His watch mate nodded, pulling out clipboards that held the weather forecasts and gale warnings.

“I’ll give an actual too,” Roy continued, “this wind is becoming nasty.”

Jack selected a pair of well-spaced remote radio stations to avoid feedback interference and began transmitting. "Securite, Securite, Securite. All stations, all stations, all stations. This is Tyne-Tees Coastguard, Tyne-Tees Coastguard, Tyne-Tees Coastguard. For gale warnings, strong wind warnings and the inshore forecast, listen channel six seven."

Given the atrocious weather he used the appropriate safety priority pro-words in his broadcast. Even as the message contents were being transmitted by Roy he was already transmitting on the remaining radio sites.

They had been on duty for just under an hour.

On the medium frequencies Cullercoats Radio could also be heard broadcasting similar warnings about the weather.

"Port of Tyne is officially closed, lads," announced Jim, walking over to the huge state board, dry marker in hand, "you might want to start preparing the updates while it remains quiet," he added, gesturing towards the state board.

Jim's prompt was absorbed as the two men diligently set to work. Jack, beard jaunty, calculated tidal information for the next day. His colleague pulled out a copy of The Macmillan and Silk Cut Nautical Almanac from a nearby shelf and immersed himself in sorting out sunrise, sunset and twilight times for the morrow. That task suited Roy well. His time at sea had been spent as a deck officer in the Merchant Navy. Jack had specialised in advanced communications in the Royal Navy. Jim, their senior watch officer had seen service on high-speed Air-Sea rescue Craft during the Second World War. The broadness of their skills match could not have been better for operating as a working team, whose first priority was maritime search and rescue.

“What about the met at half eight?” asked Jack, glancing up from his calculations.

It was one of the MRSC’s routine duties as a Meteorological Office auxiliary Observing Station. Every three hours they prepared and passed local weather reports to Newcastle Weather Centre. Something they – and their predecessors had been doing for over one hundred years.

“Let me do that, Son.” Jim sighed softly. “I want to have a word with the weather centre about what’s going on outside. I also need to remind them the stand-by Precision Aneroid Barometer needs calibrating too.”

Jim had been officially designated as the custodian for all of their meteorological equipment and logs. It remained the property of the Meteorological Office who wanted to ensure the MRSC’s weather reports were of the high accuracy they demanded and expected. The equipment inventory he was responsible for was both comprehensive and of considerable value. It included a Stevenson’s Screen and its impressive array of thermometers, some of which could be read remotely from inside the emergency planning room.

“I’ll take over channel sixteen when Jack’s finished his calculations,” said Roy. “We’re gusting eighty-five now,” he continued, without taking his eyes off the anemometer.

“What’s the steady reading?” asked his boss.

“Sixty-five to seventy, I’d say. We’re up to hurricane force. The forecast says severe gales, gusting storm.”

“OK, thanks,” said Jim in a business-like way. “Looks as if the DC will be spending his maintenance budget on roof slates!” he continued with a slightly vindictive cackle. “I suppose we can always collect the ones that blow off and use them instead of paper with chalk,” he went on mischievously.

"That would stop him whinging about our excessive use of stationary," he further helpfully suggested, eyes twinkling.

"I'd appreciate a relief soon anyway," cut in Jack, "nature is making calls on me."

Maintaining the distress watch, he was tied to his desk. Without needing directions from their boss, the watch officers seemed to be almost casual about changing places at half past eight, just before Jim went out to do the met. With the best, copper plate hand writing of the watch, relieved of the distress desk Jack would also write up their prepared information on the state board. His immaculate handwriting was just one of his specialist skills that was unique to their watch. He was also the only touch-typist among them.

Jim was happy to wait until the duties were duly swapped by his junior colleagues. After pacing around the operations room, trying to make sense of the increasing fury of the weather beyond its windows, he retreated to the emergency planning room to complete the weather observations for 2100hrs just as he left, the anemometer recorded a gust of ninety knots.

When he returned to the operations room ten minutes later, Jim quickly realised with some irritation that his two watch officers were discussing shipping casualties that had recently occurred.

"Didn't you know some of the crew who went down on the Herald of Free Enterprise when she sank off Zeebrugge in March?" remarked Jack, almost casually.

Roy, now also clad in a headset nodded, speaking through his desk's internal intercom.

"It was quite a close maritime community in Dover when I was doing seasonal work there on the ferries," he replied. "I remember her appearing on the scene as a new ship. The Spirit of Free Enterprise was the first of their class, then came The Herald, followed by The Pride. Leggoland we used to call them, due to their odd appearance!" He quietly shook his headset clad features. "Recently there was also an inter-island ferry that sank in The Philippines with a large loss of life. I was reading about it in Lloyds List. Is it too much to hope that's it for this year?"

Jim gave a warning growl. "Can't you two lads find something better to talk about? You ought to know that you are tempting fate discussing such things in this weather!"

Any chance of further conversation was immediately cut short before their boss could chastise them further by Newcastle Weather Centre telephoning for their meteorological observation. The two other men shrugged and Jack quietly continued with writing up the state board.

Peace returned to the operations room until just before nine o'clock when the incoming call buzzer sounded on the RDCE desks. One of the green private wire lights illuminated showing that Cullercoats Coast Radio Station wanted to talk to them.

"Evening, Cullercoats." The Yorkshire accent was informal, but clear and jaunty, like its owner's beard.

Jack had automatically reached for a pad of CG15B message forms, self-carbonating, in quadruplet, the top being coloured pink. In one well-honed movement he had retreated from the state board, picked up the call and swung into his chair.

The conversation continued for a couple of minutes, before he finally said, "Right-ho, I'll have a chat with our boss."

His expert scribing, another well practiced skill, meant he stopped writing as soon as the call was finished.

"A bit of a strange one, boss," he announced as the building shuddered again and the anemometer needle rose past ninety-five knots. "With the deteriorating weather Cullercoats thought we might like to know that they think a ship may be having engine problems off shore. They used MF R/T to call a French Coast Station, but Cullercoats reckon they could be in VHF range; here, off The Tyne."

"Anything else?" asked his senior watch officer.

"Not really. Everything was conducted in French. The operator at Cullercoats thinks he was making a radio link telephone call to an agent or superintendent to report a problem. I suppose everybody seems to be getting jumpy about the wind."

"Otherwise, he wouldn't have bothered us," responded Jim, sighing audibly. "Does the ship have a name?" he asked, slightly exasperated about the lack of forthcoming information.

"Aye," responded Jack, briefly consulting his notes. "She's called Chapelon."

Without having to remove his headset, Roy, as channel sixteen operator propelled his wheeled chair rapidly back from his desk, grabbed a weighty volume of Lloyds Register of Shipping from a book case immediately behind him and started turning the pages towards the ship's name.

"She's a multi-purpose general cargo ship," he said, scanning the information on the page in front of him. "Registered in Dunkirk, French built, French owners and no doubt a French crew too."

The wind crashed and shrieked with added fury around the building, loosening the first roof tile as the anemometer recorded this new gust in triple figures. Damage had already started occurring on houses lining the sea front between Tynemouth and Cullercoats. The operations room lights then flickered ominously. For now, the emergency generator remained silent. Jim started thinking, weighing probabilities.

"Try raising him on sixteen, Son," he finally said. "I don't suppose he'll want to answer; with us being office bound foreigners."

Roy grinned at his boss's acid comment and started writing in his log as he selected the Tynemouth transmitter and depressed his foot switch.

"Chapelon, Chapelon, Chapelon, this is Tyne-Tees Coastguard, Tyne-Tees Coastguard, Tyne-Tees Coastguard on Channel Sixteen, over."

His eyes scanned the radio direction finder display, hoping there may be a reply. Nothing. He repeated the call twice more, before writing N/R, short for 'No Reply' in the comments section of his log book. Their substantial building then almost seemed to crack as it shuddered again under another massive gust impact. This time its occupants observed with slight concern a window that was seen to bow in a little as the wind's ferocity intensified. The mean speed was in excess of eighty-five knots and the gusts were getting dangerously close to the one hundred and twenty knots maximum reading on the anemometer. The fault panel on Jim's desk suddenly and briefly shrilled as an alarm showed problems at the remote radio site at The Heugh, near Hartlepool, before self-correcting and resetting itself. Roy briefly sat back in thought. If a ship had any sort of difficulty in this, they really needed to know. There was one unusual protocol that might solicit an answer, but it had been a long time since he had spoken a word of French.

Glancing at his watch mates his formulated plan made him feel a little self-conscious and nervous.

“One last try,” he finally said.

Jim, who was normally reticent about looking for trouble gazed intently at the anemometer and nodded his agreement. His sixteen operator took a deep breath and depressed his foot switch again.

“Chapelon, Chapelon, Chapelon, ici Les Affaires Maritime De Royaume Uni, si vous voulez repondre sil vous plait?”

His two colleagues instantly gazed over, mouths agape in astonishment.

Nothing. He felt somewhat relieved, but at least he had tried.

Then, after a seemingly long pause, cautious and clearly highly suspicious, a voice quietly drifted across the ether and into the operations room. “Oui?”

A green line flashed across the radio direction finder screen and a bearing placing the Chapelon almost East by South of The Tyne was recorded on its digital display.

“I’ll work him,” Roy called across to his colleagues.

Jim, double checking to make sure the channel sixteen receivers were activated on his desk nodded, muttering that English was supposed to be the international maritime language. Roy instinctively knew that along with his very limited French he also needed to play the diplomat in order to win the confidence of the voice somewhere beyond the horizon.

“Ah oui, bon soire, Chapelon. Je m’appelle Tyne Tees Coastguard.”

Making sure he made it a request, including the word please, he directed Chapelon to Channel 67, their main ship-to-shore working channel.

As Chapelon’s operator switched and responded on their working frequency, the tone of the French voice had clearly resigned itself to British Bureaucracy.

Reaching for his own pad of CG15Bs, Roy had already activated Channel X-Ray on his RDCE Desk drawing a deep and unsure breath. Channel X as it was designated, allowed the selection and use of several VHF frequencies. In this case he had punched the sixty-seven button as he tried to start thinking in French. He was committed; as he quietly reflected that the Frenchman might be a little casual with his radio procedure but at least he didn’t whistle at you; a habit common to most fishermen.

Roy introduced himself as informally as radio procedures allowed him to the operator on Chapelon commenting on the wild weather. With concern in his voice, he asked whether the ship and her crew were safe?

Chapelon’s third officer spoke slowly and carefully, aware that the coastguard he was talking to was struggling with his native language.

In the operations room Roy’s colleagues watched in silence, intrigued at a skill neither of them knew their workmate had as he started to struggle with a language he had not used for years. The previous occasions had been when he had worked on ferries sailing out of Dover and his French speaking ability, even then, had never been that great.

On Chapelon's darkened bridge, with the ship rolling heavily and sickeningly to beam-on seas, the third officer was also only too aware of the master and chief engineer standing next to him as he spoke to the voice ashore. The master had already commented about the terrible French coming over the radio receiver and his mood seemed worryingly foul. Chapelon's great man was annoyed. He felt perfectly able to deal with their minor problem without involving United Kingdom Authorities. Having deliberately instructed that the earlier call in English should be ignored, being hailed in their own language from a 'roast beef' had been something of a surprise to say the least. The third officer meanwhile, automatically and naturally reverted to speaking at his normal dictation speed as he explained their defect. When he finally released the transmit button, there was a noticeable and pregnant pause.

The distant coastguard begged with him to slow down, having barely understood anything. His plea brought laughter to the bridge breaking the obvious tension in the air. The terrible accent that drifted across the airwaves that seemed indifferent to grammatical rules was almost endearing. The master felt his annoyance thaw as he started to feel a little warmth with that distant, pleading and friendly voice. He ended up deciding to take the VHF radio hand set himself and tried to explain the problem, slowly and simply. There was another pause before the coastguard said he thought he understood their problem before asking Chapelon to stand-by. As their ship lurched in horrendous seas, the bridge team huddled around the VHF radio set intrigued to hear what would be said next and whether the coastguard operator had really managed to understand them.

In the operations room Roy was concentrating so hard with his new task that he was unaware of his colleagues still staring at him, mouths agape, as he rummaged in his briefcase for a small and battered French to English dictionary, originally bought in Dover and that he was now studying, whilst scrawling on the CG15B. Finally, he keyed the radio transmitter again. As he spoke, grins spread across the faces of everybody on Chapelon's darkened bridge.

He said perhaps he understood, before adding he thought they had a fire in their exhaust, adding, "En Anglais, a scavenge fire."

The chief engineer nodded his head vigorously, unseen in the darkness and grunted approval. The man at the other end of the radio clearly knew something about low-speed diesel engines.

"Oui," the master responded, in the affirmative.

Chapelon's crew had never heard their language being massacred with such finesse before as the questions kept coming, but the coastguard was making himself understood as he got into his stride, speaking in what would never pass as his second language.

As 'the coastguard' asked for their position, the third officer quickly worked the variable range marker and bearing indicator on the radar, confirming Chapelon was thirty-six miles off the Tyne with the river bearing two six four degrees.

And still the questions continued as Roy the coastguard desperately scribed turning French into written English. Forty-one men on board bound to Grangemouth from Dunkirk.

"Oh la la!" Roy suddenly exclaimed, expressing sympathy that they had left their home port just before Christmas.

On Chapelon's bridge, in the glow of the radar screen and instrument lights, the master, chief engineer and duty watch looked at each other in astonishment. The man ashore seemed to be able to read their minds and feel their sentiment.

"Oui," responded her master, trying to keep the conversation simple, adding that it was not so good.

Then Roy asked about their bunkers, referring to them as petrol and then asked for black and white.

Open laughter now echoed around Chapelon's bridge. He could have been a wine waiter taking their orders. The chief engineer had the figures in his head allowing a fast response from the master as he told Roy they had six hundred and forty-five tonnes of heavy fuel oil on board and seventy-eight tonnes of marine gas oil.

A general radio conversation then followed concerning any dangerous goods they were carrying. Chapelon's master shuddered as he wondered whether a full manifest was required, but Roy whose name remained unknown to them for present, seemed satisfied with the fact they were carrying three hundred tonnes of classified dangerous cargo.

Making his voice more business-like, Roy concluded by briefly saying perfect and thank you, before adding he was listening on Channel Sixteen and Sixty-Seven.

As soon as the radio exchange was over, Chapelon's bridge staff started to rapidly confer among themselves. Their call with the company's duty engineering superintendent had clearly been intercepted. They guessed correctly, when they assumed it had been by Cullercoats Radio, who had then made a report to the coastguards. The operator they had spoken to at Tyne Tees Coastguard, despite his laughable French, obviously knew about merchant ships. They speculated correctly that he must have sailed on them himself. It was also obvious his concern was primarily about their safety in atrocious weather and he immediately knew a scavenge fire, whilst being an inconvenience, was no show stopper.

The master, who's foul mood was steadily lifting said he was happy to keep in direct contact with him. Everybody then heartily laughed when the duty quartermaster cheekily enquired whether they could give him some tuition in their native language too.

Unexpectedly, the chief engineer suddenly wagged an admonishing finger. He had warned them slow steaming was likely to upset his scavengers. As he nearly lost his footing on the rolling bridge, the master, became instantly irritated again. This time with his near equal and curtly told him to shut up!

"Give me a chance to finish writing this lot," said Roy, relieved to be talking in his own language for a change as he concentrated on his notes.

It was the unusual and intense silence from his two colleagues that made him instinctively and briefly look across at them. Both were staring with a mixture of amazement and laughter in their eyes. He felt his face flush with colour.

His boss's Northumbrian accent seemed to be exaggerated when he next spoke.

"Now, Son, you sit comfortably while I get you a Cognac and a Goulloise." He chuckled mischievously.

Jack's Yorkshire also seemed stronger than usual too, when he said, "Aye, do we need to issue a health warning to the snails in the castle grounds as well?"

As Jack quickly picked up a telephone call from Humber coastguard and roared with laughter, it seemed they could not resist getting in on the act too.

Still scarlet, Roy finished his scribing and finally looked across at Jim.

"Do you want a verbal briefing or a copy of the log?" he asked pointedly.

His boss leaned back in comfortable contemplation in his chair.

"Provided you stick to English, Son, I'm all ears!"

"Alright. General cargo ship, Chapelon, not under command in heavy weather thirty-six miles off The Tyne. Bound Grangemouth from Dunkirk." He smirked slightly when he said, "We have a language problem. Forty-one men on board, I have her bunker figures and she has some dangerous cargo on board. The vessel is currently disabled from a scavenge fire. She should be under way again in about fifteen minutes."

His boss digested the information.

"OK, thanks," he said once more and suddenly becoming business-like in his reaction. "By the way, what exactly is a scavenge fire?" He asked.

Roy looked up from a small chart table, also within reach of his desk, where he was plotting Chapelon's position, still clad in his headset. He quickly glanced at the entry in Lloyds Register, nearby.

"Don't forget I was a deck officer, not an engineer," he stated. "Chapelon is fitted with a two stroke, low speed Sulzer marine diesel engine. For some reason, they seem to be more prone to fouled scavengers then B & Ws and other similar engines. I suppose scavenging describes the removal of exhaust gasses and unburnt fuel from the engine's cylinders. Sometimes, treacle like liquid deposits build up around the scavengers. Heat and combustion can then set them on fire. A bit like a chimney fire, I suppose," he said, shrugging his shoulders.

The Chapelon's chief engineer would no doubt have winced at such a comparison.

"Provided you stop or slow down the engine," he continued, "the fire should burn itself out, with little or no damage resulting."

"For a non-engineer, you seem to know a hell of a lot about it," remarked Jim.

"When I was a cadet, I did my week in the engine room with a Sulzer," he replied. "It was fitted with flap exhaust valves and following a scavenge fire I was given the job of scraping the burnt-on carbon off one of them."

"And no doubt it helped enormously with your character building," retorted his boss, offering no sympathy about the incident whatsoever. "Given the weather, I'll give the DC a heads up," he continued with a sigh, halting the general discussion abruptly. "He is our duty officer over Christmas. By the way, haven't either of you noticed the anemometer's packed up?"

"Well reporting that to the Met Office is your job, not ours!" was the gritty response from Jack getting a dark look from his boss as a reply.

Without warning, the operations room was briefly plunged into darkness and the alarms on Jim's desk squealed as the tempest intensified outside. In addition to the slamming and howling wind; waves breaking against the cliffs over one hundred feet below them could be both clearly heard and felt.

“Sitrep to DC,” announced Jim a couple of minutes later. “He’s to be informed if the ship doesn’t get under way in half an hour.” Chuckling, he added, “He also asked about his precious roof slates.”

“Do you want that logging?”

“No!”

Ten minutes later Chapelon was hailing Tyne-Tees Coastguard on the radio to announce she was under way at slow speed again whilst turning her head into the weather. Given there was no chance of her building up to her full-service speed in the awful conditions, her chief engineer had obdurately insisted they should burn marine Gas Oil for the remainder of their passage to Grangemouth. For once, her master readily agreed. What her owners might say about the extra expense was an open and unanswered question.

Optimism could clearly be felt coming over the air waves when Chapelon called Tyne-Tees Coastguard again to report she was resuming her passage and had increased her engine power. Speaking in French, there was obvious relief in Roy’s voice too, before he asked whether they were suffering untowardly in the intensifying weather.

Her master informed him all was well with the ship. Amazingly it was too, despite the battering they were suffering. Everything important on Chapelon seemed to be intact, unlike the chaotic scenes in cabins, the galley and dry store rooms beneath their feet.

“Bon,” responded Roy briefly, before asking them to stay in touch, still worried there may be further problems.

As Chapelon’s master replied, a background thud was suddenly audible over the open radio channel.

"Hell, that sounded like an explosion!" shouted Roy, alerting his colleagues to a new, potential problem. "Chapelon, Tyne Tees Coastguard!" His spoke with firmness and urgency.

Chapelon immediately announced she had stopped again, finishing with 'Attendre s'il vous plait,' as she asked the coastguards to wait.

"Something else has happened out there," Roy warned his colleagues. "The ship has lost power again."

The normal, relaxed banter, a signature of their watch, instantly ceased. Like a dog searching its prey, Jim, the senior watch officer seemed to sniff the air. Beyond the warmth of the operations room windows the duty watch looked out as lights were being extinguished in Tynemouth and Cullercoats, succumbing to failing electrical supplies as they too were at the mercy of the violent elements. The same scenario was occurring on the south side of the river as the whole electricity grid started showing weakness and vulnerability. Their own substantial building was now constantly being battered and buffeted, groaning under the strain on its exposed headland. What it was like for Chapelon in atrocious seas without any power, they hardly dared guess. Then their lights went out and stayed out, as electricity was finally severed to the MRSC. Ten long seconds later, the emergency generator automatically started and restored the building's functions. Jim quickly updated his station log carefully noting the time.

"Tyne-Tees Coastguard, Chapelon." Her master's voice had a sound of weary defeat to it.

Frowning and brow furrowed, Roy had trouble understanding the problem before realising there had been an explosion inside their main engine and correctly anticipated the cause. He then immediately asked whether any of the crew had been injured by the latest setback.

Her master replied in the negative. Up on Chapelon's bridge, lines of strain were starting to etch themselves on his face as it was suddenly slammed home that the friendly and at the same time uncannily competent voice speaking terrible French ashore had become their lifeline and source of potential help. They needed no further convincing that the coastguard's primary, possibly their only concern was their ship's welfare. For Chapelon's master, the thought brought a glimmer of comfort in a situation where control could easily be lost. The increasingly crushing responsibility he was having to face was being shared by somebody who appreciated and understood his situation. Feeling a little guilty he realised he had never really thought a great deal about the British Coastguard or their vital role before; but then he wasn't alone, very few people did. That was until their search and rescue skills were suddenly needed.

Roy sucked his teeth and turned to his boss.

"They've suffered a crankcase explosion," he said in a flat voice, "no reported injuries."

"How so?" asked Jim.

"You have to remember that low-speed marine diesels have huge spaces inside them. If you get a build-up of combustible gasses that ignite, then an internal explosion results."

"Can it spread? What about damage?" asked his boss with interest.

"Well…" Roy hesitated, drawing on his limited working knowledge of marine engines that was now being pushed to its limits. "Above the engine room bed plates are a series of crank case inspection covers. They are supposed to displace should an explosion occur, to act as relief valves and minimise damage to the engine. That's why I asked about people being injured. Clearly nobody was near them when the explosion happened. We now need to give Chapelon's crew a chance to inspect for internal damage and report back."

"Why did the explosion occur?" continued Jim, his curiosity further aroused.

"I really couldn't tell you. It may be related to the scavenge fire, it could be a coincidence. The cause could be any number of factors that allowed a build-up of combustible gas within the engine's internal spaces."

"What now?" The way the question was asked, meant Jim expected an immediate reply.

"We need to wait for them to complete their inspection and report back." Roy paused before speaking again. "If we are lucky, she may be able to proceed under limited power. At worst it will be a dockyard job."

"How come our cars don't blow up?" asked Jim suddenly and unexpectedly. "Given their general state?"

"Similar things might occur," replied his junior. "The physical space within their engines prevents anything approaching violence. The massive internal spaces in a low-speed marine engine means there is room for the explosion to expand and become considerable."

"Thank you, Son," he finally said. "I'll phone the DC again when we get more information from Chapelon."

They waited for a full fifteen minutes, taking the opportunity to make another brew and complete writing up the state board for the next day. Jim grabbed a red marker pen and started filling in details about the 'casualty' on a separate board that he pulled into position on its wheeled frame. Pacing and measuring their nervous energy during incidents was something that had to be learnt and practiced. People who found such skills impossible to grasp, usually found their emotions became quickly exhausted and rapidly burnt out in the specialist working environment the three men inhabited. Such people did not last long when exposed to the demands made by the operations room floor.

Chapelon's chief engineer had been heard cursing freely when the lurching deck had thrown him into the door frame as he waddled off the bridge. That he was now changing into overalls and joining his team down below indicated the potential severity of the problem. Her master remained on the bridge, thoughtful and silent, sensing the movement of his dead ship as she laboured beam-on to the awful weather. He carefully moved around to the chart table to study the nautical chart resting on it. There was no doubt in his mind that beyond the western horizon, the good people of Tyneside would be getting on with their Christmas celebrations and preparations. That, and the thoughts of Dunkirk were now becoming of little consequence. Minutely studying the littoral area on the chart, he finally managed to locate where Tyne-Tees Coastguard Station was located, just north of The River Tyne entrance. His body relaxed a little as he let his thumb rest on the chart symbol. He now knew that here were people who would do everything in their power to help him.

Meanwhile, unseen below the master's feet, the chief and second engineers started feeling their exposed skin being scorched by hot metal as they briefly clambered into the Sulzer with powerful flashlights through the now fully removed crankcase cover that had been distorted by the explosion.

Number Three Unit was a mess. The explosion had driven the unit's piston hard against its cylinder head. In the process, it has struck the exhaust flap valve and thrown it back into its scavenger. The piston had suffered irreparable damage. Worse, the connecting rod's big end was distorted. The retaining bolts were jammed tight and the bearing shells shattered. Hidden damage didn't even bear thinking about. Number four unit had also suffered as a result of collateral damage too. Repairs were almost certainly beyond the capability of the ship and her crew, even had the weather been calm. The chief engineer briefly touched his naturally sullen deputy's shoulder and offered words of comfort. Unable to do anything to remedy the situation, Chapelon's chief engineer went to personally phone the bridge.

Cocooned in their warm and bright operations room, the coastguards hadn't just been busy with their routine tasks and sipping hot drinks. They had alerted Lloyds Intelligence Service in Colchester enquiring about potential salvage tugs in the area. The immediate response they had received was not helpful. There was nothing within one hundred miles of Chapelon other than harbour tugs. The severe weather meant they were an option that could probably be ruled out. Anything else that might have been able to realistically help Chapelon was too far away and involved with the off-shore, North Sea industry – and having a hard time trying to carry out their own responsibilities.

"Tyne Tees, Chapelon." Roy responded quickly and clearly to the call on Channel Six Seven.

He had already anticipated what was coming by the tone of the master's voice.

Her master's voice now sounded weary and defeated as he relayed the ship's desperate plight.

Roy responded appropriately using his limited French carefully and keeping his voice neutral. He tried to offer encouragement when he told the ship that they were actively looking for 'souvetage' – salvage options. The words of comfort, given the lack of tugs, somehow seemed inadequate, but it remained necessary to re-assure Chapelon that they were working on her behalf. Glancing up at the operations room clock, he realised it had been half an hour since the ship had passed her position as he immediately asked for an update on her location.

There was a short pause before Chapelon's master responded, waiting while his third officer worked the radar's electronic curser and variable range marker again. He then stated that the Tyne Entrance was now bearing two six seven Degrees at a range of thirty-two miles.

"Repeate!" Roy seemed to shout the request in an astonished, knee-jerk reaction.

The reply was carefully repeated. He demanded that Chapelon wait as he waved at Jim for his immediate attention.

"I need to get this plotted," he said urgently, "but this guy is drifting towards the coast at eight knots. At that rate he will run aground at between half one and two in the morning!"

"I'm onto the DC now," responded Jim. "We need to start talking directly to the towage brokers we have on file and get back to Lloyds Intelligence to stress the urgency."

Jack pulled out a file and set to with a determined will. Jim's telephone conversation with their duty district officer was extremely brief.

"The district controller is on his way in," he announced.

This time, there were no wise cracks about roof tiles.

"I'm about to brief Tynemouth lifeboat's hon sec too," he continued.

Five minutes of rapid, noticeable activity followed and yet still nothing suitable for towing Chapelon had materialised.

"No joy from either Lloyds or Samuel Stewarts," announced Jack. "Given the weather, the nearest salvage tug is at least twelve hours away."

"Check with the port authorities to see whether there is anything suitable in the Tyne, Wear, Tees or Blyth," sighed their senior watch officer, "and stress the urgency!"

There was no point in checking with Forth or Humber Coastguards for their respective estuaries. They were suddenly running out of time.

"What about that new broker, Marint?" asked headset clad Roy, "it will probably be negative, but you never know."

"Give them a quick ring, Son."

Jim knew they were now getting desperate for salvage options.

"Where is he likely to ground?" He continued.

"North of the Tyne, say between Blyth and Amble. We'll know for sure later. Do you want me to get fifteen-minute positions off him?"

Jim nodded as his 'dedicated' radio operator also telephoned Marint.

Just over ten minutes had passed before the district controller, soaking and windswept strode into the operations room. Of medium height, plump and balding, but otherwise with neat greying hair, he was clearly in his late fifties. His uniform reefer jacket, with its three gold stripes and unbuttoned was revealed as he took off his soaking wet weather guard. He wore a naturally cheerful expression that matched his rotund body. He watched in fascination, at a conversation that was taking place over the radio in French.

"I can smell the garlic from here," he commented smiling, as the conversation finished.

"Is this going to be the theme for the night?" enquired Roy in exasperation as he turned to plot the latest position on the chart.

The district controller meanwhile had already turned his attention to his senior watch officer for a full briefing, glancing at the state and casualty boards from time to time.

"Tugs?" asked the district controller.

Jack, almost habitually and briefly studied his CG15Bs before answering.

"I can confirm there is nothing that will get there on time to prevent Chapelon running aground. We are still looking," he added.

The DC nodded.

"Does Chapelon's master appreciate the gravity of his situation?"

Jim turned to his French voice for an answer.

"Yes, in that his disabled ship is taking one hell of a pounding in weather the likes of which we've never seen before – and no. I don't think he fully appreciates that in a few hours, Chapelon will be battered to pieces on the rocks."

"All of you," announced the district controller, "is Chapelon in grave and imminent danger?"

The two junior members of the watch let their boss speak for all of them.

“Grave yes, imminent, not quite yet.”

His colleagues nodded their heads in support.

“Do we need a competent French voice in here yet?” he asked. “We need to impress upon Chapelon her situation.”

Jim leapt to Roy’s defence.

“No! the language problem is being worked around, but most importantly, a good rapport has been established with Chapelon. If we get an interpreter in, it needs to be in an advisory role only.”

“Agreed,” said the district controller. “I’ll go to my office and brief region. Get on to RCC and have them bring a helicopter to immediate readiness. Find out about a nimrod too as overhead comms could be useful. Make sure they are fully briefed about our weather – and while you’re at it, enquire about the duty warship or any other naval assets that might be of help from Flag Officer Scotland and Northern Ireland, FOSNI.”

He was thinking on his feet.

“How about a sitrep?”

“On to it, boss,” replied Jack. “The pro-forma’s on the screen and is already about one third completed.”

He pointed to the VDUs of their recently installed ATS Telex system. The first real introduction of Information Technology that had been placed in coastguard operations rooms.

“Good man,” replied the DC. “Try and get a brief one off as soon as possible.”

With that he left to talk with his duty regional controller.

When he returned a few minutes later it was obvious the operations room had stepped up yet another gear.

"We won't have a nimrod for at least three hours," announced Jim. "The duty aircraft is already on a tasking in the western approaches. The standby aircraft is being prepped and its crew alerted."

"Duty warship?" asked the DC.

"A frigate, alongside in Plymouth," was Jim's response, "nothing else."

"The duty officer was apologetic but people are on their Christmas Leave. It will be daylight before anything can be rustled up out of Rosyth. Given Chapelon's drift, Rosyth is too far away anyway."

"Helicopter?"

"The Boulmer crew has been called to readiness."

Jim had a detectable smile on his face. He was ex air force. Like Jack, his bearded watch officer, the DC had been a specialist communicator in the Royal Navy – and their old service had been unable to offer help.

"How about Tynemouth Lifeboat?" asked the DC, pointedly ignoring the hint and guile at inter-service rivalry.

Jim became business like again.

"You can see on the state board she's up in Jarrow. The honorary secretary has agreed to put her on Immediate Readiness. He's getting a crew out to her as we speak. The weather is the big concern. He will discuss the risk of tasking her with his own operations room in Poole. You can see the port is closed. Simply getting out of The Tyne will be a problem."

"What about the other boats?" asked the DC.

"If our Arun can't make it, should we really consider risking the Waveneys' at Blyth and Hartlepool and the old double-enders elsewhere, including Amble? Poole will need to call the shots on that one."

As Search and Rescue Mission Co-ordinator, Jim was thinking ahead with the resources he had available – and thinking clearly.

"What's Chapelon's drift? How far off is she, where is she likely to ground and when?" asked the DC, striding over to the small chart table and the plot being maintained there.

His junior, headset clad colleague swivelled in his chair.

"She is less than thirty miles off now. Divergence on her drift is a little erratic. I still think she will ground between zero one thirty and zero two hundred hours if she continues to drift unhindered. As to where? North end of Druridge Bay probably," he said, tapping the relevant part of the chart with his dividers.

"Christ almighty!" exclaimed the DC, "she could ground on Coquet Island!"

"I was thinking the same" was Roy's quiet reply.

He deliberately directed his next comment towards his boss, Jim.

"Does that mean we should consider her in grave and imminent danger?"

Both the senior men looked at each other and nodded in agreement.

"See if you can get her master to declare he's in distress," said Jim pointedly.

A reminder that he was still the search and rescue mission co-ordinator – and should remain so, unless formally told otherwise, despite the DC's concerns and enthusiasm.

Roy, as sixteen operator thought for a moment before hailing Chapelon, conscious that his district controller was standing behind him – and that he was also a stickler for correct radio procedures. He raised the ship in text book fashion before reverting to his far from textbook French. He explained to Chapelon's master that their 'commandant' was in attendance and they needed to talk urgently about his predicament.

"Oui."

They clearly had the master's full attention.

The district controller watched open mouthed as Roy spoke with Chapelon's master in his own language, explaining that he was likely to ground in three to four hours and there was no hope of salvage, concluding that the risk to the ship and her crew was very grave.

Chapelon's master immediately realised he was having the facts spelt out to him in a decisive and uncompromising fashion. The bad French and the hard, factual tone now in the coastguard's voice seemed to ram home the situation that he was likely to lose his ship and some of her crew. His stomach felt as if it was being twisted in knots. He suddenly felt clammy and slightly dizzy. The coastguard then unexpectedly and forcibly asked him to declare a distress situation immediately.

On his darkened bridge, the ship's master felt himself reeling back from the VHF set while he stared at the dimly lit instrument in horror. He didn't need telling that his ship was in difficulty but even without power she was riding the seas well and was not in apparent or immediate danger. In the engine room, the third engineer had found his second wind, as following his persistent nagging, he, the second and their colleagues were struggling to lift the cylinder head off Number Three Unit using the overhead crane and chain blocks to steady their work against the ship's roll in a dangerous, desperate, but realistically unlikely last-ditch attempt to get some sort of power out of their shattered Sulzer. Even with the spare piston and liner they carried, they knew they had the odds stacked heavily against them. Despite the now obdurate persistence from the coastguard ashore; for Chapelon's master, the thought of declaring a distress situation seemed defeatist and final. He was filled with dread. It signalled the ultimate in professional humiliation.

"Je ne sais pas," he finally stammered across the airwaves, his voice filled with uncertainty.

Roy responded almost automatically, telling him to standby, as he turned decisively towards his district controller and senior watch officer.

Chapter 4

Mayday Relay

"He's stalling and I think I know why," Roy declared to his colleagues, "his indecisiveness probably means he needs time to fully appreciate his predicament. Unfortunately, such a luxury is no longer available."

"I have a feeling I know what you are angling towards," announced the district controller looking at his junior operator thoughtfully.

Everybody in the operations room was clearly and independently coming to the same conclusion.

"Let me talk to region." He finally sighed, selecting an outside line and grabbing a spare telephone handset on the senior watch officer's desk.

Roy, with authority in his voice commanded Chapelon to wait, as their district controller made his telephone call. On the bridge, her master almost meekly did as he was bid, still stunned by the coastguard's suggestion that they were in distress. Slowly, very slowly, he too was beginning to appreciate how rapidly events were changing for the worse. All the ship's crew around him were now becoming visibly apprehensive as the reality of becoming shipwrecked in weather that would probably be fatal finally hit home.

“Somebody make sure they record this with a date / time stamp,” demanded the district controller as he replaced the telephone hand set in its cradle and pushed the line cancel button. “The Duty Regional Controller agrees that we should declare a distress situation on Chapelon’s behalf.”

With that the operations room was about to enact a recently agreed protocol that had been formulated following the loss of the Penlee Lifeboat in the south west of England. Penlee had not been the first recorded incident where masters had shown reticence to declare distress when faced with grave and imminent danger. Jack had already reached for a Form CG15A, their distress pro-forma and was filling in the relevant section with a well-practiced hand. Jim meanwhile was activating the private telephone line to Cullercoats Radio.

“Aye, that’s right,” he finally said to the astonished operator, “can you broadcast on 2182 and Five Ton please.”

He paused and listened to coast station operator’s reply before saying, “Fine, thanks.”

“We will telex the details over as a flash message.”

While Chapelon was listening on Channel Sixteen, Roy spoke directly to her, explaining carefully the protocol they were about to instigate.

Without pausing he suddenly, almost unexpectedly for the listeners on board Chapelon said, “Break, break. All stations, this is Tyne Tees Coastguard, standby for Mayday Relay broadcast. I repeat, stand-by for Mayday Relay broadcast! It’s all yours,” he said to Jack, as he released his foot operated transmit switch.

Jim reached for a telephone line, first speaking to Jack who already had his headset clamped across his crown.

"Include Tynemouth Lifeboat and a rescue Helo in your information number one please."

Without pausing he spoke into his own boom microphone.

"Hi, Hon Sec? Request immediate launch, Tynemouth Lifeboat to MV Chapelon, twenty-five miles east of The Tyne. Forty-one souls on board. Wind at the river mouth is estimated to be one hundred and twenty knots plus with high, confused seas. All communications on Channel Sixteen, a distress situation is about to be declared."

He paused as the honorary secretary spoke briefly.

"Yes, we will inform the port authority, given they have closed The Tyne. Let us know once you have spoken to Poole as to whether the launch is approved."

He was making notes on his own CG15B. The district controller had pressed the direct private telephone line button to RCC North and requested a helicopter scramble. He then appraised the Northumbria Police control room, who were already feeling overwhelmed and under increasing pressure, dealing with an influx of calls and incidents resulting from the mayhem the storm was creating overland.

Jack looked across at Jim.

"Ready," he said simply. "Local, Gare and Hauxley?" he asked, indicating the transmitter stations he thought of using.

"Bang it out on the lot," injected the district controller. "There's always a long chance something might be passing that can get a tow line on Chapelon."

At least their network of remote radio sites was still working, albeit with alarms screeching and then resetting. Already, some of the sites were relying on their emergency, back-up power. *How long would they keep going for?* wondered Jack as he selected their local site, along with

Newton and Whitby for their first transmission. His skill as a highly trained radio operator shone through as he pressed his foot switch.

"Mayday Relay, Mayday Relay, Mayday Relay, this is Tyne-Tees Coastguard, Tyne-Tees Coastguard, Tyne-Tees Coastguard. Begins, Mayday. Chapelon, Information Number One. MV Chapelon Call Sign Foxtrot Sierra X-Ray Tango, disabled and adrift in extreme weather twenty-five miles east of The River Tyne. Immediate towing assistance requested. Forty-one persons on board. Tynemouth Lifeboat launching, rescue helicopter requested. Tyne-Tees Coastguard co-ordinating, date time group 242225 UTC. This is Tyne Tees Coastguard."

He keyed the remaining radio sites and started transmitting again. The operator at Cullercoats Coast Radio Station recorded the message and without the need of any confirming telex started to transmit on 2182KHz, before reaching for his morse key and doing the same on 500KHz.

Chapelon's plight had been formally upgraded and she was now the subject of a full-blown search and rescue mission.

Chapelon heeled over as the forces of the wind and weather hammered into her.

Thankfully, at least her auxiliary services were being maintained, even if her massive Sulzer had probably breathed its last. As he gripped a grab-rail in response to the rolling deck, her master realised that once again the coastguard had stepped in when on this occasion he had felt dismayed and paralysed by their predicament. It was a massive help to the planning and preparations he had to do now. Professional, skilled specialists who were clearly adept with marine distress protocols were sharing his increasingly heavy fears and burdens. He briefly wondered whether their help and guidance should make him feel guilty, but instead he felt immensely grateful. His overloaded mind had briefly and understandably stalled, given the developing and never before experienced pressures that came with the certainty he was going to lose his ship. The breathing space the coastguards had given him allowed him to think again in the way a ship's captain should. He had mentally noted the distress transmission on their behalf, understood the pro-words, but little else of the English transmission. It didn't matter. Tyne-Tees Coastguard were handling the communications in their native language – and the more he worked with them, the greater became his confidence in their professionalism and capabilities.

"Mayday, Chapelon, Tyne Tees Coastguard," the now familiar voice was calling, "mayday Tyne-Tees Coastguard, Chapelon."

Communications protocols learnt long ago were coming back. The coastguard explained that now that Chapelon was in distress, all communications would remain on Channel Sixteen.

"Oui," responded her master, simply.

As he continually dusted off a nearly forgotten language, Roy was able to confidently explain they had not yet found a suitable salvage tug but were still looking. He then advised them that Tynemouth Lifeboat was being launched and would be departing shortly along with a rescue helicopter. Finally, he asked Chapelon's master to prioritise who should be the first to abandon his ship.

The master responded without hesitation. He was getting well used to this man's way with his native language and called the mate over, noting that now all his deck officers had quietly appeared on the bridge. They needed to consider the initial evacuation of all their non-essential personnel. How could they safely achieve that in the fearsome deluge that roared unabated beyond the protection of the wheelhouse? It was a challenge that needed careful planning, even with specialist search and rescue units that would be coming to their aid. His seamanlike instincts knew that for the safety of their entire crew and ship, what they still desperately needed was a tow line and a powerful tug. It was the one thing the coastguard had been unable to locate, yet they refused to give up. The master then briefly and ominously thought about possible towing contracts. He had no time to haggle and any tug's captain, all whom inevitably seemed to have a buccaneering spirit about them, would undoubtedly and gleefully push for the greatest financial imposition possible. What if unlimited demands were made of him? With Christmas now dawning, being able to contact his owners quickly with outrageous salvage demands was questionable to say the least. He may be obliged to go it alone and risk his entire career.

"Mayday, Chapelon, Tyne-Tees Coastguard."

Somehow, the master realised that those people at Tyne-Tees Coastguard seemed to be able to read his troubled mind. Roy was speaking in the master's own language again as he uncannily expressed his concern that a tug master might put impossible demands on him for his tow line, given the urgency of the situation and there was little leeway to quibble.

That may include the dreaded Lloyds Open Form. Roy decisively suggested that *he* should talk to their owner.

Chapelon's master felt both relief and apprehension at the suggestion. He was also forced to briefly and reluctantly leave the bridge to go down to his office. On his return he passed a private telephone number for the ship's owner to the coastguard over the radio. Glancing across at the radar's planned position indicator he saw with some shock that the radar's range scale now showed they were less than twenty-four miles off the Northumbrian coast and the potential for their total destruction. With every sweep of the time, the base line, now illuminated land, showed a heavy orange glow on the near-by screen.

That they were also slowly drifting to the north of The Tyne was also obvious without the need of a bearing indicator for measurement. The master briefly thought about the ship's owner who he knew well and guessed correctly would be understandably shocked to hear he was likely to lose his ship. His earlier telephone link call had been to the duty engineering superintendent. It had been nothing more than a routine report to say the ship had been stopped as a precaution because of a scavenge fire in heavy weather.

They had merely been obeying company standing orders that specified procedures should be followed when a ship had problems in near gale-force conditions or above. He was also extremely glad that Tyne-Tees Coastguard would make the call. In part, because he knew their owner who could also display a remarkably a short fuse and was more likely to agree to the principle of a financially detrimental towing contract with a state maritime authority rather than with him, the owner's legal representative on board. Such unilateral action, even in desperate circumstances had cost many a master his career.

In the operations room, following Roy's suggestion, a short, sometimes slightly heated debate followed, concerning contacting Chapelon's owner directly. Finally, the district controller decided to discuss their intentions and reasons with their duty regional controller and with Lloyds Intelligence in Colchester from the privacy of his office.

"You had better make the call," he said without ceremony to Roy on his return, "the regional controller is now in the operations room at Yarmouth. He won't come up here yet, not in this weather; he could be held-up for hours. Then he would be no use to anybody. It is also time to get an interpreter into the operations room too," he insisted. "See whether we can find a couple more staff to come in to reinforce your team as well," he finally added, before deliberately moving close to Roy.

He lightly touched the man's shoulder.

"No disrespect to your efforts," he continued in a surprisingly gentle tone, "you have done well, but we need more fluency."

His watch officer sighed through lines of strain already etched on his face.

"I'm grateful," he said simply.

To the west of Paris lies the stylish suburb of Vaucresson. Unlike the storm battered north east of England, Christmas was about to break on a town that was nestling under a brilliant, star-studded sky. Already, the ground was crisping with frost. Conditions that truly reflected the festive season.

Chapelon's owner and his family lived in a substantial, but stylish white painted, detached property, almost block like in shape, nestling in neatly manicured grounds that were discreetly hidden behind equally neat hedges. Warm, friendly lights, muted by drapes, reflected on lawns already turning white with frozen moisture. Within, and surrounded by tasteful, festive warmth, family and friends had assembled and were enjoying bonhomie, drinks and finger food in a large drawing room where a beautifully decorated and illuminated tree added its pine fragrance to the atmosphere. They had all elected to attend an earlier evening vigil service in their local parish church before returning home to offer and open their gifts and presents. Not an unusual custom in many European countries on Christmas Eve. Soon, when it was midnight, they could toast the sacred day and then consider retiring for the night.

It was the live-in maid who answered the insistent ringing of their telephone located in a lobby close to the drawing room. She had already detected the assembled party was resenting its intrusive sound and Chapelon's owner, whose short fuse she knew all about, had glowered at her slowness to react. She attempted to be discreet and deflect the demands of the voice speaking terrible French at the other end of the line, but his stubbornness was winning through. Finally, when she was threatened with 'Les Affaires Maritime de France', she went with some trepidation to disturb the head of the household. With a disparaging glare at his unfortunate maid on whom he was heaping blame for this unexpected and unwelcome intrusion, he strode over to the telephone, muttering that he had duty superintendents that were quite capable of dealing with his fleet.

"Oui!" he answered gruffly, almost shouting into the receiver.

The voice at the other end was choosing his words carefully and clearly struggling with the French language, explaining he worked for the United Kingdom Maritime Authorities at Tyne-Tees Coastguard. Roy then asked him to confirm he was Chapelon's owner.

"Oui," he answered in a bad-tempered voice, wishing he could throttle the Englishman at the other end of the line.

Being interrogated during Christmas by his own authorities was bad enough; this was beyond belief! Dealing with petty bureaucrats was what he employed staff for!

"Vous est parle l'anglais?" Roy asked hopefully.

"Non."

Chapelon's owner was ready to roar expletives at this intruder and slam the telephone down.

Roy's voice suddenly became harsh and stubborn when he announced that Chapelon was in distress in terrible weather, brutally adding they needed to discuss salvage options urgently.

Chapelon's owner's eyes widened in astonishment and his pupils slightly delated in shock. It was the last thing he was expecting to hear. Especially given the still, crisp weather outside his residence. He asked Roy to wait, his voice now showing sudden urgency and concern as he went to find his daughter. The young lady was home on vacation from university, where by good fortune she was studying languages.

In her early twenties, the owner's daughter was both intelligent and confident. She wore a well-fitting and fashionable dark dress, that was both discreet and at the same time flattering to her figure. She had enjoyed being the attention of the male members of their gathering in particular;

flirting expertly. She had also inherited her father's short fuse and was angry when she saw he was clearly both distressed and upset. She grabbed the telephone handset with a purpose and spoke sternly.

"Who are you and why are you upsetting my father?"

She noticed that the family matriarch was now staring seemingly vacantly at a painting of Chapelon that adorned the lobby wall along with other ships in his fleet; both past and present.

Roy seemed to ignore her barbed comments and continued unabashed.

"I am a duty officer with Tyne-Tees Coastguard. We have very little time. Your father's ship Chapelon is in grave and imminent danger. A distress situation has been declared and we are in the process of dispatching a lifeboat and helicopter to her."

The young lady instantly felt her confidence and brashness subside. Unwittingly her grip on the telephone receiver tightened.

"I–I don't understand," she managed to stammer.

"I will explain then," replied Roy sharply. "Chapelon has broken down east of the River Tyne, in weather that is worse than anything, any of us have ever known. Conditions are extremely bad. The wind is probably blowing at over two hundred kilometres per hour and pushing her towards the rocks. She is likely to run aground in two- or three-hours' time. The ship will then become a total loss. That leaves the problem of her crew and trying to keep them alive."

She suddenly found herself whimpering slightly in an involuntary, shocked reaction. People, some of whom she knew may be killed, as the impact of Chapelon's probable fate struck home hard. Roy now had her full attention. She briefly turned to her father, who himself was clearly in shock before speaking into the telephone again.

"What do you need?" she fought to avoid stammering as she spoke.

"We really need a sizable salvage tug," came the reply…

"Wait." She could hear radio traffic in the background.

"Mayday, Chapelon, Tyne Tees Coastguard."

The owner's daughter, whilst trying to force herself to remain calm and collected, found herself choking back tears as she recognised the voice of the ship's master. Marine VHF communications meant she could barely understand what he said. Meanwhile her father started watched the mounting drama and his daughter's watering eyes with rising dread. Behind him, the sounds from their party had discreetly stopped as people stood close to the lobby, watching and listening. She clearly heard Roy asking Chapelon's master to wait as he spoke into the same microphone to which she was connected advising him he was in discussions with her father. She was suddenly startled to realise he was talking to her again, without even pausing for a breath.

"I must get back to this problem quickly. We need a salvage tug, we have used all our resources to find one but to no avail. We are still looking, but time is running out. Will you please ask your father, that should a tug be found, whether he will agree to whatever salvage contract, including a Lloyds Open Form that may be demanded by the tug's master to get a towing line rapidly on to your ship? It is the only way to save your ship and the best way to keep her crew alive and safe."

Tears were now openly pouring down her face as she relayed the information to her father who had turned pale, before providing the coastguard with his answer. She tried to regain her composure before speaking.

“My father says he will accept any contract. He does not care about his ship any more, but please, save her crew.” She started sobbing quietly.

Roy’s voice softened. When he spoke again he was being gentle.

“Rest assured, the safety of your ship’s crew is our primary concern, we will do everything in our power to keep your people safe but with this weather it will be challenging, it will be difficult.

“Please can you keep us informed?” she suddenly pleaded.

“I can’t promise that,” was Roy’s response, “we are busy, but if you have fax or telex, we can copy you our sitreps – situation reports. They are in a set format, but they should help you understand what we are doing.”

“We have fax here,” choked the owner’s daughter.

She found a pen and wrote quickly as Roy passed the operations room number.

“OK, we will send you a message that will include our number,” she finally said.

She replaced the telephone receiver and wept openly and unashamedly. Nothing in her short, competent and confident life had prepared her for this desperate situation, where the lives of forty-one of their compatriots, some of whom she had met, were at stake. She felt hopeless and helpless. They could do little to influence the developing, desperate situation and had become totally reliant on other, unknown and distant people who had promised their all.

In France, Christmas Day had almost arrived. Ironically, a few minutes later, the duty marine superintendent telephoned Chapelon's owner, having received a disturbing message from the French Foreign Office and Lloyds Intelligence, concerning his ship.

"Chapelon's owners have agreed to any salvage contract," Roy explained to his colleagues, "could they also receive copies of sitreps?"

The district controller thought for a moment and nodded his agreement, with the provisory that any loss of life would have to be reported through appropriate authorities. He had noted the haste with which his watch officer had responded to Chapelon's call and emphasised the pro-word Mayday. It clearly had the right effect.

"Mayday, Chapelon, Tyne Tees."

Roy succeeded in explaining that Chapelon's owner had agreed to accept any salvage contract, provided of course they could locate a salvage tug in time.

"Tynemouth lifeboat is about to launch," announced Jack who was now demonstrating his skills with dual headset working both efficiently and competently, with an open telephone line in one ear and Channel Zero in the other.

Two minutes later, the lifeboat started calling over the radio on Channel Zero that it was launched on service. Their crew list was passed, each individual having his own number that would confirm his name. Jack automatically responded with a time check and an updated situation report. He also passed the latest weather forecast.

He paused before adding, “We will try to determine what is going on between the piers and let you know. The forecast doesn’t tie in with this.”

The lifeboat’s coxswain gritted his teeth and he felt that was an unnecessary understatement! The boat hadn’t even reached ‘The Gut,’ marking the beginning of North Shields Fish Quay and she was already slamming into a swell being driven up the river. For now, in restricted waters and under foul conditions, whilst staying below himself, the coxswain had two experienced crewmen conning the boat from the flying bridge above him. Soon, they would clear the decks of their Arun Class Lifeboat and batten down, well before they reached the open sea. Other members of her crew were already starting to feel their stomachs rebel as the seated coxswain tightened his seatbelt in the wheelhouse and created his own special fug, contentedly puffing on a massive pipe. As he began to sense his boat’s increased reaction to the elements, he knew that simply getting out of the entrance between the Tyne piers was a challenge that would demand all of his seamanship skills. Beneath his feet, the boat’s twin engines growled with powerful reassurance. Every ounce of their muscle would be required when the moment came.

The district controller parted hanging blinds and stepped up to the darkened lookout platform in front of the operations room. He became immediately aware of the raw power of wind, spray and rain as it battered the heavy, sloping, double glazed windows around him. The whole structure of their building seemed to groan and creak in response to the elements. The platform was uncomfortably cold, despite near-by radiators working on full power. He went over to a corner that overlooked the river mouth. As his eyes adjusted to the dark, he made out the shadowy bulk of their tripod mounted Dopple binoculars. Claimed as war reparations by somebody with foresight from the Kreigsmarine at the end of the 1939–1945 conflict, these powerful glasses with their limited field of view were of no use for his intended task. Instead, he found a pair of 7X50s on the window ledge. For a good minute, he carefully studied the scene outside, seeking the Tyne breakwater entrance through blinding spray and spume. His detailed local knowledge of the river and its surrounding area was now essential. Striding back down into the operations room, he called out to both Jim and Jack.

"Tell the lifeboat I can't see the Herd Sands Beacon or South Pier Light at all. What I can make of the North Pier Light is worrying. Green seas seem to be breaking right over it. The pier around it is totally awash. The seas in the river entrance are high, confused and breaking."

He had used the sweeping beam and lume of the powerful North Pier Lighthouse to try and determine the reality of the situation at the pier heads. It had been far from easy.

"Keep them on Channel Zero until they are well clear Son," injected Jim.

The tasking was high risk and an open, uncluttered communications channel with the lifeboat was absolutely essential.

Before the lifeboat had even reached the Herd Sands on the south bank of the river and well up from its entrance, the coxswain had called his flying bridge crew down to the wheelhouse, taken the boat's con himself and had the wheelhouse door closed and securely battened down. The boat was riding the seas like a big dipper as she powered into the teeth of the ferocious wind. Her crew, now all strapped in themselves, let their bodies swing with the boat's motion in their matt-black painted wheelhouse. They were now grateful for the drab colour as it minimised reflection from their instrument lights on the widows and fittings. With their low mounted antenna, the radar screen was a mass of sea clutter. Blowers were working at full power as the crew attempted to keep the windows clear of condensation. The Arun briefly cork-screwed and the coxswain expertly applied counter-helm as a green sea swept right over the boat. She then seemed to shake herself and continued to power towards the now converging breakwaters that guarded the entrance to the river. The infamous Black Middens, that had claimed the lives of many a seafarer and wrecked countless ships before the piers and breakwaters were built were now left to port and astern of the lifeboat's throaty exhausts.

The whole crew was tense as they approached the gap in the breakwater that marked the start of the North Sea proper. The powerful North Pier Lighthouse was above them clouded in sea and spray but remained a help to the coxswain as he prepared for the challenge ahead. The radar, despite rain and sea clutter corrupting its picture, offered a little, limited help. This close to the shore, the Decca Navigator was useless for their exit from the river. They continued their plunging journey towards a frightening mass of confused, raging and breaking seas. Two of the crew were now retching into buckets and the coxswain's teeth clenched down hard on his pipe as the boat slammed into the maelstrom marking the river entrance. He pushed the throttles to their stops, as searchlights picked out a world that seemed to have gone primevally mad. Their brilliant beams were suddenly reflected straight back into the wheelhouse from the roaring, white water around them. They were quickly extinguished. The seas slammed into their starboard bow dangerously pushing the boat to port. The coxswain put his helm hard over and eased back on the starboard engine. The boat responded well and suddenly the piers and the river entrance were astern but the conditions remained relentlessly vicious and dangerous.

The boat's bows suddenly plunged deep into the water and kept on plunging – and then another sea slammed her side, just as the props, rising clear of the seas screamed as the stern lifted high into the air. The vicious, relentless wind continued to push the boat beam-to the seas into a full broach as the coxswain tried to counter with a for-now useless helm. The bows lifted, the stern slammed back into the sea but it was too late, even as the coxswain fought against the elements and their predicament with all his skill. The combination of ferocious wind and sea continued to slam the boat onto her beam ends.

The brilliant red glow of an alarm light suddenly flooded the wheelhouse with its urgent message. A warning horn blasted – and then, as the engines automatically cut-out, Tynemouth Lifeboat capsized.

There was instant confusion in the cabin as the boat took them through a fearful manoeuvre. Everybody was suddenly hanging in their straps with their legs heavy, being pushed by the weight of gravity. Loose objects, including the vomit from seasick crew swirled around them. The chart dividers evilly stabbed somebody in his ear. The boat seemed to hesitate in a crazy turbulent world with her keel showing among the waves. Then the expertise of her design showed through as she continued her roll and self-righted still beam-on to the weather. Shocked with the rest of his crew, the coxswain instinctively reached for the engine starter buttons. He was only too aware that they were now north of the river and in danger of being battered against the cliffs beneath the Coastguard Rescue Centre. The engines groaned but failed to start. Ignoring her savage motion, the boat's mechanic athletically swung towards the engine-room hatch and disappeared down below. Seconds later, the port engine coughed into life giving the boat something to fight back against the elements with. It helped her crew shake themselves into action, nursing cuts and bruises. Meanwhile, the starboard engine remained reluctantly silent. The coxswain picked up his VHF Radio microphone. That didn't want to work either. The capsize had completely stripped the wheelhouse roof of its fittings including the boat's aerial array. His voice sounded weary as he grabbed a hand-held radio and called Tyne-Tees Coastguard. He briefly considered whether to send a couple of crews out on deck to assess their damage. As well as his radio aerials, he wondered whether the Arun's dinghy; their Y boat had been washed away too. As his boat briefly tried to be a submarine, he rapidly put that thought to one side. It would have to wait until they were in a safe haven. There was no way he was going to attempt to return into The Tyne, even on two engines, let alone one. He would struggle towards the shelter of Blyth to the north.

"Tynemouth Lifeboat has suffered a capsize just after she left the river," announced Jack in a straight, matter-of-fact voice, whilst nervously stroking his beard. "She's trying to make Blyth on a single engine, no serious injuries to her crew. Judging by her comms, I guess they are having to use a hand-held radio. Do you want me to let the Hon Sec know?" he asked Jim.

"Please, Son," was the response, as Jim took a deep intake of breath, "keep her on Channel Zero and keep a close eye on her. Five-minute safety checks. We need to get another sitrep out and update the Mayday Relay to Information Number two as well. If they are not on the sitrep address list already, make sure RNLI Headquarters at Poole are recipients."

"Right, you guys get on with the telephone comms and mayday update," announced the district controller unexpectedly, "I'll issue the new sitrep."

Like Jack he was a touch typist who had also ensured he had kept fully up-to-date with their new ATS Telex system.

"I'll do the updated Mayday relay and concentrate on Channel Sixteen," said Roy.

He paused and added, "I should really inform Chapelon in her own language that she won't be getting lifeboat assistance once the Mayday Relay update has been broadcast."

Jim, glancing at his district controller, who was busy on the telex keyboard and not taking his eyes from the Green ATS Telex VDU, decided to put a call through to the regional controller himself. His team may have been on overdrive, but they were working smoothly and thinking clearly. As Jim spoke, Mayday Relay Information Number Two was being broadcast, the DC was pressing the 'send' key on the telex and the first of many safety checks was being made with Tynemouth Lifeboat as it battled north up the coast towards the safety of Blyth.

"Briefly, everybody," he suddenly decided, "let's see where we all are, I'll start."

The DC turned towards him with a look of total approval mixed with pride on his face. Tactical management was being carefully maintained.

"The RC knows about the lifeboat. He has clearly instructed that no more launches are to be requested by any of us. Any attempts or considerations for further launches must be sanctioned solely through the honorary secretaries and RNLI Headquarters at Poole. He has also approved us getting extra staff into the operations room. He remains concerned about the safety of the rescue helicopter and Tynemouth Lifeboat."

"Tynemouth Lifeboat is proceeding towards Blyth on one engine. Other than cuts and bruises, her crew are OK and remain battened down in the wheelhouse," said Jack. "Her honorary secretary is understandably both worried and concerned. He confirmed he will sitrep Poole with a verbal briefing and will discuss reception arrangements for his boat with the honorary secretary at Blyth. He also said he will tell Poole that there should be no more attempted launches until the wind abates to storm force. Two colleagues who live in Tynemouth village should be here in a few minutes. Station Officer Plans is on his way in too but has warned that even from Whitley Bay, where he lives, getting in could be problematical. The chef from the local French restaurant in Tynemouth should be with us soon too, to provide an interpreter service. By the way," he flippantly added, getting a scowl from the district controller. "I understand Christmas telly has packed in."

"Sitrep's on its way," confirmed the DC. "I'll have another chat with the RC shortly. He is likely to want the Marine Pollution Control Unit alerting and he can get

Yarmouth or Humber to do that. We need to consider pushing a minimise signal out to the coast for routine traffic. If he agrees, Humber can do that on our behalf too. Well done all – and thanks."

"Mayday Relay Information Number Two has been broadcast," said Roy, glancing up from his console. "Chapelon is now less then eighteen miles off-shore. Unless there is a change in divergence from her drift, I still think she will ground at the north end of Druridge Bay. I've told her Old Man that should a tug be found, that Chapelon's owner has sanctioned her taking a tow line, come what may! Unfortunately, the provision of towing assistance still remains academic. I've just double checked with Cullercoats Radio. The responses from suitable tugs to their MF broadcasts places the nearest, realistic craft at least eight hours away, particularly given the weather out there. Her crew's best hope now, is the rescue helicopter. I'll be briefing Chapelon's Old Man as a priority."

"OK, thanks all," said Jim, "let's get on with it. When our first reinforcements come in, get them to put the kettle on," he suddenly pleaded, "we know the emergency generator can take it!"

He reached across his console for the direct telephone line to ARCC (North) keen for an update on the rescue helicopter.

North of Tynemouth, in Rural Northumberland, RAF Boulmer was operating on emergency power too as they manned up for their rescue helicopter tasking. Air traffic's anemometer had suffered the same fate as the one at Tyne-Tees Coastguard and was now useless. All they could advise was that wind speed across the airfield exceeded one hundred and twenty knots. Simply trying to walk was hazardous and often practically impossible. In 202 Squadron's hanger, one of two yellow search and rescue sea king helicopters was being prepared for her tasking. Both her flight and ground crew were worried. Once the aircraft's two gnome gas turbine engines had been started, it would be necessary for the aircraft to engage its main rotors. That operation alone would be both difficult and hazardous, quite apart from how they could achieve a successful take off!

Serious thought had already been given to starting the helicopter within the shelter of its hangar, engaging rotors and then taxiing out, such was the concern about the effects of the tempest outside. A drastic procedure, but it was a case of balancing risks in an extreme situation. Flying directly into the wind as she struggled out to Chapelon, the helicopter's ground speed was going to be excruciatingly slow – and should they even be able to make it out to the disabled ship, safely winching the crew from her would be challenging in the extreme. It would require at least three trips in all to recover her personnel. At some point the aircraft would also have to refuel.

For now, their first task was simply getting safely off the ground. Clad in their olive-drab flying suits, bright yellow helmets at their side, the four members of the helicopter's flight crew in the end decided to start engines and engage rotors outside in the lee of their hangar. Despite Christmas leave commitments, extra ground crew and air base staff, accompanied by the stand-by flight crew had joined to help prepare and position the aircraft with their collective specialist knowledge and sheer muscle. The nose wheel tow bar had already been attached and a tractor was connected. The aircraft's crew climbed on board and the hanger doors were opened. The whole structure had already been rattling and shaking against the onslaught of weather and people were even having to shout above the noise inside, but nothing had prepared them for what lay beyond the hangar's shelter. The wind, shrieking almost at right angles to the open doors, seemed to be trying to physically suck everything outside. People hung on grimly grabbing what they could for support as they felt the Venturi effect from the driving air trying to drag them with it. The noise of the tractor's engine starting was almost totally lost among the crescendo of other sounds. On board their rescue aircraft, the four-man crew grimly pulled on their helmets and strapped in. The captain, sat in his right-hand seat, nodded to their crew chief outside, as they started to ready the aircraft. With crew stationed around the aircraft to steady it – and each of its five rotor blades being controlled by men with hooked poles, the procession began to move towards the gaping doors and the fury of out-of-control weather waiting to greet them.

The aircraft bucked and heaved, but was carefully manoeuvred by many willing hands to the lee side of the hangar. Even there, swirling wind eddies continued to rock the airframe and pepper it with debris. More people helped to steady the wildly gyrating rotors while the captain indicated he was ready to start the aircraft's turbines.

Spooling up was undramatic. The engines started in their usual, no nonsense, efficient fashion. The rotors and airframe were then cleared of personnel and with a much-practiced routine, the rotors were engaged and started turning. The airframe shuddered and juddered, but at least maintained its stability. The winch operator did his checks in double quick time, monitoring the operation of his principle life-saving device, from which he derived his title, before sliding closed the aircraft's main access door and strapping in.

The two pilots had already decided to briefly taxi directly into the wind, just clear of the hangar, before opening the sea king's twist grip throttle wide and pulling on the collective for all its worth, to make a clear break from the ground. It was a sound plan, probably the only option available, given the weather they were fighting. They knew that as soon as they were airborne, driving rain and debris would guarantee that their visual references would disappear and they would be immediately flying on instruments. Carefully they released brakes and initiated their plan by taxying the aircraft under her own power. As soon as they reached their chosen take-off position, the captain opened the collective mounted, twist-grip throttle wide against its stops and started pulling on the lever it was attached to with all his strength to get the aircraft flying…

A massive gust of wind, that could have never been foreseen, raced across the airfield and slammed into the hanger. That in turn, created a vicious, local wind sheer. The Sea King, already light on its wheels, as its rotors torqued up and strained as they started to take the helicopter's weight, was hit broadside on with a hammer blow; below the rotor hub, where the gear box was carefully cowled. The crew immediately felt the aircraft lurch sideways. Her captain slammed the collective back down as both pilots desperately worked rudder pedals and their cyclic controls to try and correct an increasing sideways roll. Amid a tortured, terrifying noise that outdid the elements, the rotors struck the concrete apron and tore themselves apart. In their chaotic, sideways leaning cockpit, the pilots reached up for their emergency engine stops and fuel cut-offs. Their eyes scanned the fire alert panel that stayed thankfully passive. The splintering carbon-fibre parts of the rotor blades disappeared on the wind. The depleted uranium mass balances in the rotor tips, the same material armoured piercing shells are manufactured from, made use of the energy created by the impacting rotor blades and took off on their own destructive trajectories. Two, punched through the hangar wall, one exiting harmlessly through the other side. The other arrowed straight into the standby helicopter ripping through vital lines and services rendering that aircraft un-airworthy too.

Held firmly by their straps, the Sea King's crew were shaken, but unhurt, as they felt and heard their aircraft, now a useless and inert object, thrown onto its side, become a plaything for the weather, as it ground and bumped over the concrete and tarmac. It felt as if the ferocious winds were mocking them. In a burst of anger and frustration, the helicopter's captain let out a choice expletive, before slamming his fist in pent-up fury and frustration on the now vertically pointing – and redundant instrument glare-shield in front of him.

Jack took the call from ARCC (North). His voice spoke with its same, forced calmness, relaying the impact of the news, as he continuously speed-wrote.

"Both helicopters have gone U/S at Boulmer," he announced flatly. "The duty aircraft keeled over before she left the ground and her rotors touched."

His colleagues didn't need any embellishment to picture the resulting chaos *that* would have created for her crew.

"The stand-by aircraft has been damaged by flying debris inside the hangar. She was pierced by one of the rotor mass balances."

He quickly noted; 'Sitrep DC & SWO', on his log before putting his pen down and briefly taking off his headset to rub his face.

"Any chance of another aircraft?" asked Jim, more in hope, then conviction.

His colleague looked across at him and shook his head.

"Not in this weather," he added. "The transit times would be too long to get out to the ship, from either Leconfield, or Lossiemouth," he said. "ARCC are reluctant to involve Boulmer as a staging post in any tasking given what has just happened. Not until the weather abates."

"By then it will be too late," muttered the DC.

"I'll let Chapelon know," Roy said, with just a hint of weariness showing in his own voice. "Update to Mayday Relay Info Number three?" he asked Jim, who nodded.

"Belay the update!" commanded the DC suddenly as he stepped over to the massive state board and started to study it.

At that same moment, the operations room door opened and the first of their extra staff stepped in, his features battered by the atrocious weather outside. Jim, briefly ignoring his DC's demands, grinned broadly in relief.

"Put the kettle on, there's a good lad!" he enthused.

"Wets all around?" enquired his freshly arrived colleague. The response was an immediate gaggle of vigorously nodding heads.

Chapter 5

Muster the Coast Rescue Equipment

Like a conductor drawing his orchestra to order, the DC turned and faced his three duty coastguards, seated in front of him at their desks.

"Muster the Coast Rescue Equipment!" he demanded.

It would be their final, last-ditch gamble to save Chapelon's crew, calling on their own specialist resources and volunteer personnel stationed along the coast. They would be working with obsolescent, some might have said obsolete equipment in a last desperate roll of their metaphoric dice.

"Which teams?" enquired his senior watch officer pointedly, as a sharp reminder he was still in charge of the operations room, as he glowered at his boss.

The DC briefly apologised as Jim cleared papers that covered a list of pager codes beneath his desk's Perspex.

"Let's go for every mainland team north of The Tyne," he said in noticeably consolatory tones, nodding and acknowledging he was not trying to steamroller Jim's authority with his own enthusiasm. "And don't forget the VLB here at Tynemouth. Get the teams to load everything they can. When Chapelon runs aground we will need to get her crew off with Breeches Buoy. I want every Eighty-Three

Millimetre Rocket Launcher, rocket and line available up in Druridge Bay, along with the Schermuly pistols and Forty Millimetre rockets and lines. Get them to empty their stores. All the extra lighting, cliff gear, tools and cordage – and more importantly, all the manpower we can find!"

He strode over to the chart press, opened the draw containing ordnance survey maps and grabbed the sheet that covered Druridge Bay.

"The National Trust car park at Druridge Bay is sheltered by dunes," he continued. "If we have to ram open the barrier with a Land Rover, then so be it. We can quote our authority under the Eighteen Ninety-Four Merchant Shipping Act, given this is a wreck service. That will be our initial assembly point," he added, thinking aloud, "Until we determine the exact location of Chapelon's grounding."

Jack selected a telephone line and put a call through to the volunteer duty officer for Tynemouth Volunteer Life Brigade. The brigade, fully equipped and manned to conduct coastal rescues and searches had opted to remain independent from the Auxiliary Coastguard Service and other, similar teams. It was historically appropriate. Nearly two hundred years before, a generation prior to the coastguard service's birth, an incident occurred where a ship had stranded on the near-by Black Middens in atrocious weather – and with that came a dramatic change in thinking. The good people of Tynemouth had lined the shore nearby with wrecking and plunder in mind. Instead they became moved by the plight of her crew who were all lost. It was the impetus to form a volunteer brigade that could rescue personnel from stranded ships. They adopted the then new Breeches Buoy and Manby line throwing mortar as their main means of rescue and were pioneers for a change of mind-set that would spread across the whole of the United Kingdom – and beyond. Their independence and proud history was more than justified.

Jim punched in the call out code for Berwick-upon-Tweed Coastguard Rescue Company, selected an appropriate radio site and sent out the pager tones on Channel Zero.

"Full call-out for Berwick Coast Rescue Equipment" was his following transmission on Channel Zero.

He knew that many of the team members kept their radio receivers open. They would be on their way. He then selected Seahouses to continue the routine.

Along the length of the coast of battered Northumberland adrenaline started pumping in response to the pager alert tones. People by the score motivated themselves for action. For some it seemed slightly surreal, almost disbelieving. Those who were monitoring Channel Zero on their radio handsets and listened to the team call out instructions rapidly appreciated the enormity of their tasks on such a filthy night, without having to be fully briefed about the situation. Many were in homes now devoid of power and suffering damage. They were already worried about the effects of the fearful conditions on their households. Their other family members, ready to celebrate Christmas, looked on with helpless concern as patriarchs and grown-up sons started to pull on warm and protective clothing before going out into the elements to face uncertainty. One man, a deputy auxiliary in charge, was also a local church warden. They had taken trouble to light their small village church beautifully with candles, once the power had failed and were starting to greet hardy congregation members who had ventured out for their midnight service.

Now there was a new, sudden and more urgent demand on his skills and duties.

At Blyth, in a unit on a small industrial estate, the coastguard auxiliary in charge listened grimly to his briefing from the MRSC. His team were already busy preparing their vehicle and trailer.

"Full call-out for a breeches buoy rescue!" he shouted to his incredulous, assembling personnel.

It had been years since the equipment had been used in anger.

"Load everything, including all the rockets. Those with four-wheel drives transport people who can't get in the MRU, the roads will be otherwise impassable in places." He briefly chuckled at an afterthought request, whilst glancing at a near-by wall, hung with photographs and trophies, portraying the team's proud history and professionalism.

This included several awards of the "Board of Trade" Rescue Shield for really outstanding duties they had historically undertaken.

"Leave a set of heavy weather gear in a conspicuous place. The DC is coming along and bringing one of the ops room lads with him!"

Two of his team were already lifting a long, strange looking object made of tubular steel that was set apart with spacers. Legs were lashed to the main frame with stout leather straps, as they hefted it onto the roof bars of their Marine Rescue Unit (MRU), the station Land Rover, before tying it firmly down. A graduated angle of elevation control, set on one of the contraption's legs gave a hint about its intended purpose. It was an Eighty-Three Millimetre rocket launcher.

The shelves of their industrial unit were being stripped bare, as equipment was efficiently transferred into the back of their MRU and other private vehicles and wagons. Their now packed and roomy trailer was ready and being hitched to the Land Rover. One of the assembled rescue company worked the chains that opened massive roller blind doors guarding the unit's main entrance. Vehicle doors were slammed shut and the navy-blue Land Rover, with its bright yellow roof, blue lights flashing and two-tone horns blasting drove out into the fury of the night. Red lettering on its side described its intended purpose; 'Marine Rescue'.

"Mayday, Chapelon, Tyne Tees Coastguard."

Roy was thinking hard about his next transmission, turning his native English into French. He explained that there was nothing available to help them with salvage or rescue and that the rescue helicopter was 'injured' and finished. Chapelon's master acknowledged grimly. Growing tension mounted throughout the ship. Their fate and destruction on a beach was now a certainty.

The district controller hovered nearby as the devastating news was delivered and whispered additional instructions to his operator.

"Ecouter, Chapelon," continued Roy, the operations room's French voice; gaining confidence, the more he used the language.

"Oui," responded her master simply.

"Interco, je repeter, Interco."

Roy had informed them that he was reverting to the International Code of Signals by forewarning them with the appropriate pro-word. The district controller gently touched his shoulder to show his approval.

"Oui, Interco," came the response.

On Chapelon, the senior cadet reached for a hard-bound book on a shelf behind the chart table and readied the document for scrutiny. Her master was both intrigued and puzzled by the new instructions.

Roy had no need to reach for his own copy of the International Code of Signals, he knew the code he was going to use, off by heart.

The International Code book provided a simple means for passing basic information where language difficulties arose.

"Bon," he continued, first of all saying his coded instructions would apply when the ship had grounded. "Golf Sierra, je repete, Golf Sierra," he continued in a clear voice.

"Oui, Interco Golf Sierra," came the immediate, almost routine reply from Chapelon's master, who then staggering against the movement of his ship, cautiously moved around the chart table to see what the decode was.

The senior cadet had quickly found the matching letters, GS and was already pointing with his finger, as his captain read the decode in his own language. For several seconds he shook his head in astonishment. It simply stated, 'We will attempt to conduct a rescue with rocket line and breeches buoy.'

He knew of the breeches buoy from his training days where its use had been discussed with quaintness. A throwback to earlier and less complicated times. Something they had to be aware of but in an age efficient communication, all weather helicopters and modern, powerful, lifeboats, a means of rescue that was obsolete. A genteel reminder of the nineteenth century, that some coastal states, including Britain still retained; one had always assumed more out of tradition than anything else. As far as the master could recall, it had not been used in anger for years. This latest development also meant there could now be no doubting the resolve of the staff at Tyne-Tees Coastguard – and their determination to see this through. They were simply not prepared to give up on them.

Whatever happened now, he knew beyond doubt that there was a stubbornness, grit and determination to see their predicament through to its bitter conclusion. He suddenly galvanised a new sense of purpose into the team on his madly rolling, shuddering bridge calling them into action. It was time to get their technical manuals and books out and start revising! They needed to review and memorise the visual signals associated with the procedure for rescue by breeches buoy. They also had to decide where they would abandon their ship from and where they would rig the main hawser and the tail block that would carry the endless whips that powered the buoy. He quickly called his chief officer over and told him to scrutinise the crew list and draft a muster sheet, prioritised for abandonment. All the crew had to dress in warm clothes and be ready with their life jackets on. He needed to get essential ship's papers and find something he could put them in for getting them ashore safely too. While they had time, hot soup should be issued to everybody. It would be warming and good for morale. Finally, he called across to the third officer and asked him to switch on the wheelhouse lights. There was no need to worry too greatly about night vision and blacked out bridges now. The second officer, typically without comment went and switched on their deck lights too. The chief engineer waddled off to see about starting the emergency generator, remotely located from the engine room, in a compartment one deck below the bridge. Their new sense of purpose was uplifting for the entire crew who had been falling into indifferent, fatal despondency.

Now there were tasks to complete and a plan for their survival. There was something positive to aim for. There was a reasonable chance they might actually live!

"North end of Druridge Bay, definitely," called Roy, carelessly throwing a pair of dividers onto the chart.

The DC briefly scowled at the act but was interrupted by a new face coming into the operations room. Still wearing the white jacket and patterned trousers of his trade and smelling of deep fat fryers and herbs, it was the chef from the local French Restaurant close to Tynemouth Village. He was followed by a keenly received man who was bearing a tray full of hot drinks. Station Officer Plans dishevelled by the deluge outside was the last of the little procession to enter.

"Good," the DC said briefly to his staff officer colleague, "let me fully update you then I'm going to get up to Druridge Bay too," he announced, "and you're coming with me," he decided, pointing to Roy.

"I'm hardly dressed for it!" Roy protested.

"Haven't you people heard the expression 'be prepared'?" growled the DC in rising irritation.

Jim forcefully interjected, feeling his own temper warming.

"Am I still in charge of this operations room or not?" he suddenly snarled. "You are being unfair! We come dressed for the operations room because that is our place of work. Anyhow, Son," he said more gently to his colleague, "You'd better go, given the circumstances, although it would have been nice for the boss to suggest it to me first!"

He removed a dark, sleeveless jumper he was wearing.

"Use this as a body warmer, it should help. I'll ask Blyth to leave an oilskin out for you. I'm sure the district controller won't mind diverting there in his rush to get up to the action."

His voice was laced with sarcasm. The DC stayed diplomatically silent. He had bypassed his senior watch officer in demanding one of his staff and unwittingly over-stepped his own strict standards.

Glad to briefly escape the atmosphere he had accidentally created in the operations room the DC produced a spare seat from the emergency planning room and showed the French Chef over to the Channel Sixteen desk.

"Who will maintain the plot?" asked the current recumbent, as the newly arrived coastguard who had just made the beverages made ready to relieve Roy.

"No problem," responded the new face who was also a trusted ops room colleague. "Give me a couple of minutes to hand-over," Roy asked the DC, who was already deep in conversation with his station officer, "and I'll be with you."

The DC nodded. "I need to brief region and get the staff car keys," he said, as the rising, but brief tension in the operations room had disappeared as rapidly as it had occurred.

"We'll then get up to the magazine and see if we can get in past the weather to load up the district pyrotechnic spares and take them with us."

Before moving from his desk, Roy made a last transmission.

"Mayday, Chapelon."

"Oui, Je repondre."

The master and his crew too were getting their second wind, now they had been given positive goals to aim for.

Roy explained he was about to leave the operations room and they now had a fluent French speaker there to help them, before adding they would speak later.

Chapelon's master acknowledged the broadcast suddenly feeling slightly sick. He had assumed the coastguard, *his coastguard,* the voice that had encouraged and sustained them for several hours was finishing his shift and going home. In a world that was falling apart around him, he pictured the man disappearing to enjoy the festive season. His job was done, now it was down to somebody else. The master knew he was being selfish and thinking unfairly, but the events that had brought urgency and distress to his ship were hardly fair either. Was he becoming just another statistic for the UK authorities? Live or die, the consequences would be fleeting in their passing.

Getting up from his desk, Roy addressed Jim, his senior watch officer.

"It wasn't my decision to abandon you."

Jim looked at his junior softly.

"I know, Son," he said, noting his departure in the station log, "look after the DC."

"Look after yourself!" responded Jack, "it's absolutely awful out there and we have another night watch. That's provided you make it as far as Druridge Bay in the staff car. I managed to get through to the police to give them our sitrep. There's flying debris, abandoned vehicles and standing water all over the place. The staff car is hardly an MRU! The police are already inundated with stuff on the land."

He turned to Jim.

"They may be able to send a vehicle to our operation in Druridge Bay, but right now they are overwhelmed with their own problems brought about by the weather. There may be an ambulance available later too, although they are currently rushed off their feet."

"We'll see," said Roy with resignation. "By the way." He was already feeling in his pocket for a penknife. "I'm going to cut a couple of lengths off the roller towel in the gent's toilet to use as absorbent scarves."

"Is one for the DC?" asked Jim, unable to conceal a smirk of delight.

His colleague nodded with mock gravity.

"Good thinking," he continued, "he's a partner in the crime now and can only complain to himself!"

The comment brought brief laughter from the assembled personnel around him.

"We need to inform customs and immigration," he suddenly said getting back to the job in hand. "Our new arrivals will probably have no identification papers on them."

The operations room suddenly came alive to a new transmission, as exhausted and battered; Tynemouth Lifeboat announced its safe arrival at Blyth Harbour on VHF Channel Zero.

"All set?" asked the DC.

They met by the stairs, outside the emergency planning room. He noticed his colleague had already fastened his Weather Guard and that he had a scarf showing.

"Here's one for you," Roy said, managing to maintain a straight face, as he offered a length of the towel to the DC. "It will act as a barrier against the wet."

The district controller nodded his thanks and was halfway through putting it on, when its origin suddenly dawned on him.

"Is this out of the gents?" he asked suspiciously.

He received a simple nod.

"It's a conspiracy," he muttered, "I can see this is going to be one of those nights! Anyway, Bonny Lad, let's see if we can get into the magazine."

They climbed the internal stairs to the top of the tower, until they were standing on the level formed of armoured steel and concrete. A heavy weather door confronted them facing directly into the wind. They could see it straining and bowing against the forces battering it and for the first time ever, water was leaking through its edges.

"If we manage to open that without injuring ourselves I doubt if we will ever close it again," said Roy. "We could wreck the integrity of the entire building."

The DC nodded.

"We'll take the station's 'ready use' pyrotechnics and get going. Bring our single man cliff gear too. The cordage, stakes and Kim Harness may come in handy."

"Mind if I take one of the hand portables from your office?" Roy asked.

"Good thinking," responded the DC. "There's a fully charged radio in the battery charger. Its case is on the window sill."

They clattered down the stairs with their loads to the 'tradesman's' entrance and entered the car park. Despite its shelter, the wind gusted and shrieked, its eddies causing litter and other debris to churn around in a grotesque circle chipping paint off vehicle sills. Beyond its entrance, it was a continuous howling, screaming, roar. Thick salt had already caked all the vehicles and they spent further time cleaning the white staff car's windows and decided that whilst there to quickly check the emergency generator and its fuel as it monotonously rumbled, providing life-blood electricity to the whole building. The DC swung into the driver's seat and started the engine. Roy buckled into the passenger seat and switched on the car's VHF radio set selecting Channel Zero.

"Use your call sign for the moment?" he asked.

The district controller nodded.

"Tyne Tees Coastguard, Tyne Tees Delta, radio check, Channel Zero."

"You're loud and clear," came the clipped response from Jack.

"You also," Roy responded. "Departing home jetty for Blyth and thence Druridge Bay."

The DC briefly smiled. Home jetty was his own unofficial pro-word for the MRSC.

It was only as they left their relative shelter that they could really fully appreciate the MRSC was a haven of light in a darkened and torn world. The old fortifications and gun emplacements to seawards offered some shelter as they swung out onto the drive. There were no floodlights now. Tynemouth and Cullercoats too were in total darkness, devoid of power. With their headlights on full beam, they groped towards the Barbican. Its short tunnel was funnelling the wind into a tempestuous, high pitched and turbine-like shriek. The district controller struggled with the controls as the car buffeted and pitched putting as much distance between them and the moat as possible. Turning into a darkened street, there was no other traffic, but plenty of debris.

"I'm going to drive up the Coast Road to Billy Mill," he suddenly said, "it will hopefully offer us a little more shelter for our trip north."

"Happy Christmas," said Roy as they approached Blyth a little later, transiting roads strewn with broken roof tiles and pointing at the dashboard clock.

The DC glanced at him and shrugged.

They arrived at the emptied industrial unit in Blyth, torches in hand to find that the power was still working. An old oilskin, devoid of buttons had been left on a table, along with a warm woolly hat decked out in the red and white stripes of a Sunderland Football Club Supporter.

"At least there are no tears in it," said Roy as he inspected the black outer garment and slipping into the 'Macham' hat whilst searching out some old rocket line to wrap and tie around his waist, in order to hold his waterproof together.

The district controller looked on in plaintive disgust at the transformation of his watch officer into a tramp-like, scarecrow figure. The old rivalries of those who lived north of The Tyne, with those to the south, particularly Wearsiders, surfaced as he glowered at the red and white Macham hat.

"Jeepers," he muttered as they headed for the car.

The final run to the National Trust car park in Druridge Bay turned into an enduring nightmare. There were frequent stops to clear obstructions and debris from the road.

Balancing and probing with a broken tree branch he had found, that now made a useful stave, Roy checked deep puddles and minor floods to find a safe path for their car. The wind clawed at his now soaking headgear but it stayed firmly in place. Finally, they were able to turn into the National Trust car park and the assembling teams.

"Good job, I've got a nice warm hat," announced Roy, unable to resist the quip any longer, as the district controller simply glowered, "by the way, I'll need an individual call sign," he said, switching on his hand-portable radio.

"Tyne-Tees Charlie" was the response from the DC as he looked at Roy's crazy heavy weather outfit. "I can't think of anything more appropriate!"

Roy desperately tried to conceal his widening grin.

"Tyne-Tees Delta arrived Druridge Bay," announced Roy to his colleagues on the staff car base set, "it looks as if most, if not all the teams have assembled. My call sign will be Tyne-Tees Charlie."

He managed to pass on his unique identifier with a straight face as the DC maintained a watchful, critical eye.

"Request Sitrep?"

Jack's radio procedure remained flawless.

"Confirming all teams have assembled. A police unit should be on scene with you shortly. The police will also be local liaison for Customs and Immigration. Chapelon is now five miles off the coast. She will probably ground on Hadston Carrs. She has all her deck lights on, report when she is visual."

"Charlie and Delta copied" was the brief response.

"Half an hour and she will be on the rocks," Roy said, turning to the DC.

Already, driving sand and spume were blasting and rocking the car. The DC looked around. The dunes might be scouring their vehicles in the style of a sand blasting machine, but they also offered shelter and a basic haven.

"Time to get organised and briefed," he said, forcing his door open against the wind.

The team leaders; the auxiliaries in charge, had found a surprisingly well sheltered spot in the lee of a large dune that surrounded them on three sides.

"Thank you, everybody!" shouted the DC, "it's one hell of a night to ask you to do this."

Somebody handed him a megaphone.

"The ship – Chapelon will ground in thirty or forty minutes, almost certainly on Hadston Carrs. We need to relocate to the north, find a suitable equipment dump, ideally, somewhere like this and set-up. By the way, one of you will have to be in overall control, who should that be?"

Blyth's auxiliary in charge was both delighted and surprised to find himself unanimously elected. Among the assembled auxiliary service seniors there had been concern the district controller might have decided to retain operational direction himself. They had totally underestimated his strategic appreciation – and his understanding of his teams' psychology.

"Tyne-Tees Coastguard, Tyne-Tees Charlie…" Roy, the operations room escapee took it upon himself to brief his own team colleagues.

"Don't reckon much on your choice of football team," remarked Blyth's auxiliary in charge, with more than a hint of a grin and a sideways glance, when the radio work had been completed.

"You people have got me into big trouble with the DC!" quipped back Roy.

The two men burst into roaring laughter, briefly relieving the rising tenseness felt by all, given the task they had been set.

"Have you got a pair of cliff rescue goggles?" asked Roy, suddenly becoming serious.

He had already taken a pair of binoculars out of the DC's car.

"I want to start looking for Chapelon – and with all this sand blowing around, it would be impossible without them."

Their brief period of light relief and frivolity was over. The hard, serious work was about to begin in earnest as people moved back to their vehicles.

They collectively drove out of the car park past the near-by Ladyburn Lake and onto the A1068 main road that ran parallel and slightly inland of Druridge Bay. A short distance later and turning right off the main road and into a side track, they emerged by a low, rocky outcrop that was distinctive from the surrounding dunes and sandy beaches of Druridge Bay. They had arrived at Hadston Carrs whose unforgiving rocks pushed out into the sea from an otherwise pristine beach.

Before they could leave the National Trust car park, the district controller waited with enforced patience and anxiety for Roy who had carefully climbed a nearby dune and was lying at its top like a military spotter, binoculars to his protected eyes.

"Nothing visual yet," he reported, cleaning the binoculars with his handkerchief as he carried a quantity of sand and water with him into the staff car.

The DC nodded as he started driving.

"Tyne-Tees Coastguard, Tyne-Tees Charlie, negative visual on Chapelon, proceeding Hadston Carrs."

"Copied" was the brief response.

The coast rescue teams had thoughtfully cleared the route of obstructions and debris for the staff car. It meant a reasonably straight run down to Hadston Carrs where preparations were now rapidly underway. The teams had already found a decently sheltered site for their equipment dump. Vehicles had been corralled in a circle for extra shelter and their search lights and headlights were being used to illuminate the visibly growing pile of specialist rescue gear. Under the watchful eye of Blyth auxiliary in charge, everything was being unloaded neatly and laid out logically for rapid access. One of the auxiliaries in charge had already nominated his team for the role of looking after this all-important and visibly growing pile of equipment.

Tyne-Tees Delta and Charlie on scene, "Hadston Carrs," announced Roy hastily to his colleagues in the MRSC.

Grabbing his radio, binoculars and protective goggles he left the vehicle without further ado, the wind nearly ripping away the open car door. There was no point in the DC saying anything in protest. His watch officer had already disappeared into the darkness and spume towards the sea, seeking a location where he could look out for Chapelon. Another set of headlights groped its way towards them. The DC waited and then briefly spoke to the new arrivals. It was a police patrol.

"Can we leave you people to deal with customs and immigration matters?" he asked the two constables in their car. "Later on, we may need to deal with pilfering from the wreck too. My people have powers to protect it under The Merchant Shipping Act, but you would be more professional on the ground. How are things elsewhere by the way?"

"Pretty busy," responded one of the constables. "A lot of damage and injuries being suffered. Also, quite a bit of our infrastructure is taking a hit. The good news is that the WRVS is on the way with a mobile canteen and that ambulance control will try to get a vehicle here in time for when the guys start coming ashore off your ship."

"Thanks." The DC managed a weak smile. "By the equipment dump is probably the best place to park, it affords a bit of shelter and will be the rallying point for everybody. By the way, should you need help with your own communications, we can relay them to your headquarters at Ponteland through the MRSC. Having you here brings more manpower, should we need it too."

"Nice to feel welcome," responded the policeman. "We can check out the quality of the products from the dear ladies of the Women's Royal Voluntary Service, when their van arrives too."

"Provided it's wet and hot, I don't suppose my guys will have any problems." The DC grinned. "I need to get on, but ask around if you need me."

The dump, as it spread out and grew was now really taking on an organised shape. Line boxes for both rocket lines and breaches buoy cordage were being stacked no more than two feet high to prevent them being blown over by the wind. That would destroy their carefully coiled contents ready for immediate deployment. The covers had been removed from a massive breeches buoy hawser, sat on a stretcher – and needing two men to carry it. Long wooden boxes containing heavy rescue rockets were grouped together, the tops having already been loosened on two of them. Portable generators were starting up, powering electric lights. Making use of an empty trailer as a windbreak, more men were tending paraffin 'Tilly' pressure lamps, pre-heating them with methylated spirits before handing out the storm proof lights with their brightly blazing mantles. Cylinders of propane gas were being connected to massive tripod mounted searchlights whose beams would penetrate the dark and spume and illuminate Chapelon when she arrived. The leather straps had been removed from three rocket launchers and their support legs had been laid out ready for immediate deployment. All around, other pieces of gear, equipment bags and haversacks were all being brought to immediate readiness.

His men, his district. The district controller felt a sudden and immense surge of pride. He had to force himself to keep his emotions in check.

The huge rollers crashing onto the beach were of sheer monumental proportions. The spray was thick and at times seemingly solid. Driven sand, whipped up foam, spume and other debris added to the scene of fury and confusion. Hadston Carrs was somewhere just to the left. It was no use trying to spot its exact location; not in this. With his goggles clamped to his eyes, finding the simple act of breathing virtually impossible whilst facing into the wind, Roy was once again lying prone in the dunes, his head just above them as he waited for the first sight of Chapelon. His goggles' surface was already becoming opaque from flying sand. He was minimising his use of the binoculars. Being not of the finest quality, the Seven by Fifties were already soaked through. More than a few seconds of use and he had to try and clean the objective lenses with his now drenched and gritty handkerchief. Daylight would later reveal they would be fit for nothing more than binning.

An intermittent glow through the spume, nothing more than that. Roy wriggled sideways, lining up the first signs of lights in the sea with a small hummock in the dunes. He would need to estimate the ship's angle of drift by sight alone; a skill practiced many times during his countless hours spent on ships' bridges when he had been on watch. He briefly raised his binoculars for a closer study of the ship almost beam on to the beach.

He quickly estimated how it filled his magnified image. Briefly, he swung out of the wind.

"Tyne-Tees Coastguard, Delta and all stations on Channel Zero, this is Tyne-Tees Charlie. Chapelon in sight, repeat, Chapelon is in sight. Estimate she is between one point five and two miles off the beach. Standby for drift estimate."

"Delta copied." The DC's response was fast and rapid.

"Tyne-Tees Coastguard copied and standing by."

"Blyth Alpha Copied, teams standing by."

"Roger," responded Roy, "will now establish direct contact with Chapelon on Channel Sixteen."

His frozen hands struggled with the hand-portable radio's controls, as he selected the correct channel.

Roy's pronunciations were becoming more fluent and confident as he spoke in Chapelon's own language telling them his call sign was now Tyne-Tees Charlie.

On Chapelon's lurching bridge, everybody could feel a slight change in the ship's movement and motion. Outside, beyond the wheelhouse windows the wild wave tops had become even more confused, creaming and breaking. With their ship totally at the will of the weather, everybody knew they were getting close to the surf line on a lee shore. The ultimate nightmare and dread for any mariner. Her master suddenly turned with a start to the new call on the VHF Set and felt some of his fear and anxiety subside as he instantly recognised the voice coming through the receiver. His special coastguard was out there beyond the stormy waters, somewhere on the land they would soon ground on, waiting to help. He briefly recalled his thoughts when Roy announced his departure from the operations room. *How wrong could I have been,* he thought to himself a little guiltily. His voice recovered some of its jauntiness as he thumbed the transmit button and gave his response.

Roy continued the conversation, telling them he had visual contact with their ship. He said he estimated they would ground in the next five or six minutes and to be ready for 'Golf Sierra' – the breaches buoy.

"Mayday, Tyne-Tees copied," came the professional response from the operations room.

Sitting next to the Channel Sixteen operator, the French chef positively grimaced at the awful use of his language as it emerged from the loud speaker on the RDCE desk.

The voice was heard again on the far desk, this time in English on Channel Zero.

"Tyne Tees Coastguard, Delta and Blyth Alpha, Tyne-Tees Charlie. Firm visual on Chapelon. She will ground on the southerly end of Hadston Carrs, broadside on and bows facing south. Grounding is imminent. I'm reverting to Channel Sixteen and will now remain on that channel."

"Copied," replied Jack. "Be advised we have lost our Hauxley remote site. Tynemouth remains fully functional and your comms currently remain loud and clear."

Fumbling the Channel Sixteen switch, Roy briefly raised his handset to his mouth to warn Chapelon of her imminent grounding.

Blyth auxiliary in charge had found his own decent megaphone on the equipment dump, along with a large, powerful flashlight. Blasted by the weather, on their return from a brief reconnaissance, two men from the Amble team had already decided upon a suitable location for the rocket launcher as Chapelon drew ever closer. An elevated dune, close to the surf with a slightly protected lip and a good flat top covered in stout tufts of grass that bound the sand together.

"Right, lads!" he shouted with the help of his electronic amplification, turning the beam of his torch towards the site. "Start positioning the gear. Use solo cliff gear stakes and lashings on the rocket launcher, lighting tripods and anything else that might blow away! Two fully equipped and tethered cliff breast rope men will provide forward assistance to evacuees, six feet in front of the jackstay tripod. Given the weather and terrain, we will use the jackstay, not the hawser. The breeches buoy will be rigged by 'B' method."

The district controller joined Blyth auxiliary in charge as close on seventy men set to with a will. They had been given tactical instructions; it was all they needed. Their knowledge and training took over.

"We have fewer potential problems using the jackstay in this," the auxiliary in charge said, briefly turning to the DC and pointing to the hawsers piled high on their stretcher boards. "As the cordage is braided nylon, rather than manila, it should flex and stretch more easily to absorb the ship's movement as she works on the rocks as well. It is lighter and easier to deploy. It will need writing off when we finish."

The DC nodded.

"Remember to keep the whips apart when you deploy, otherwise we will end up with a cat's cradle out there."

The auxiliary in charge briefly touched his shoulder. It was a good reminder. Given the combination of a mighty tempest and the adrenaline surge that accompanies any job, the simple precaution might possibly have been overlooked.

Back on Chapelon's bridge, everybody waited in an almost surreal atmosphere of tension. The ship, their home and place of work would shortly meet her end for want of a functioning engine. The bridge was warm, lights burned without a flicker, people were for now safe and dry. Soon, they would be in a desperate survival situation. The chief engineer had quietly disappeared into the engine room. The emergency generator, one deck below the bridge was providing essential services with its limited power. He would keep all their main generators on their switch board but would get all of his people out of the pit, as soon as the ship touched bottom. He knew it would be the start of Chapelon's death throes. Luck alone would most likely dictate how long the engine room remained dry and intact.

With the weather battering Chapelon's port side, binoculars in his hands her master risked opening the starboard wheelhouse door and surveyed the rapidly approaching surf line. He elevated his binoculars slightly. There were no welcoming navigation marks, no glare or reflections from friendly villages or town lights. He guessed correctly that the weather was wrecking the infrastructure of electricity supplies on the land. There was intermittent movement ashore though. Hand-held lights patchily showed and disappeared. To one side he briefly spotted a flashing, blue vehicle beacon. Nothing to truly indicate or even hint at the mass of activity taking place only hundreds of metres away from him. The hammering and shrieking noises created by the tempest, even on the lee side, was almost beyond belief. He slammed the door shut and waited.

Everything was ready ashore as people anxiously waited for Chapelon to run aground. For the moment the ship's crew were remaining sheltered, being kept secure and safe from the elements. The dump, hidden from Chapelon was flooded with light. To maintain good visibility, all illumination was being kept to a minimum on the seaward side of the dunes as people unseen by Chapelon sought shelter among them, carefully trying to observe the ship. They were like an amassed army of old, waiting in their trenches for the order to attack. Coast rescue teams crouched behind what shelter they could find. The district controller joined his watch officer as he maintained his vigil, carefully observing Chapelon's plunging and rolling hull. Blyth auxiliary in charge also appeared at his side. All around them others too were straining to observe the moment the ship touched bottom. The district controller had briefly toyed with the idea of launching parachute illuminating flares over the ship but the wind was simply too strong to allow reliable trajectories. That, along with their questionable help in the driving spray and spume, made them both pointless and potentially dangerous. He briefly glanced over at Roy with a mixture of awe and satisfaction, as black in his tattered oilskin, Sunderland Supporters hat drawn low over his head, secured with his goggles strap he ignored the battering his face was receiving, gasping hard every time he breathed against the ferocious wind. He seemed oblivious to everything else as he concentrated on the rapidly approaching hull of the crippled ship.

"She's touched!" he suddenly shouted.

As he watched the bows plunging deep into the surf they finally found the sandy bed of Druridge Bay. Their downward motion was instantly and prematurely halted as all buoyancy was lost. Pivoting on an unnatural fulcrum near the ship's fore end, the stern swung hard to starboard in the battering wind before slamming and grinding onto the rocky bed of Hadston Carrs itself. Chapelon, still rolling sickeningly and with seas now breaking over her fore section, had grounded and stuck. The coast rescue teams rapidly emerged as one out of their shelter to start fighting their own desperate and life-saving battle.

Chapelon's master had gritted his teeth every time his ship's bows slammed downwards literally praying they would strike soft sand. He involuntarily reached for a grab rail on one of the wheelhouse consoles whenever the deck tilted forwards. Suddenly, almost unexpectedly, her plunging motion stopped unnaturally. The ship's frames groaned and shuddered as she absorbed the impact of her grounding. The bows seemed to hold fast as the next breaking wave enveloped the forecastle. Some people who were knocked over by the impact were still dusting themselves off when the still buoyant stern started swinging sickeningly and uncontrollably towards the shoreline. There was no mistaking the stern grounding as it crunched hard onto the low, rocky bed of Hadston Carrs. The ship lurched clumsily as she bodily stuck fast. Thankfully, the keel held. Had Chapelon broken her back on grounding, then the odds would have been truly stacked against her crew's survival. In the engine room; bright, noisy and hot, where people were still desperately working on their shattered, semi dissected Sulzer, the chief engineer ushered everybody up on deck, engineer officers and machinists alike. Many rubbed at cuts bruises and grazes from their efforts to mend their useless engine. Only when he was satisfied the engine room had been fully evacuated did the chief turn to leave himself. But not before turning to his Sulzer and shaking his fist and shouting personal expletives and obscenities at the unfortunate and crippled piece of machinery. He had cared for it like an only child and in the end, it had delivered failure and heartache to him! He then cocked a professional ear towards the after-engine room bulkhead. Number six hold shell plating, beneath the double bottom had clearly impacted on the rocks and was now almost certainly holed and grinding itself to pieces. *How long before the double bottom tank tops are breached and the hold starts flooding?* he wondered. Then, it would only be a matter of time before the engine room was compromised too, possibly through its after bulkhead collapsing. He had no doubt the stern frame was already fatally damaged. It was time to check on their emergency generator as it continued to provide their essential services. Thankfully safe and well above the waterline, in its own compartment below the bridge.

As the chief made his way up towards the safety of a watertight door, his assessment had been unerringly accurate. The stern frame had taken an almighty impact and beating on the unyielding rocks. The after peak and other compartments were already open to the sea. The rudder had saved the cast-iron stern frame itself from total disintegration, although impact cracks were now spreading along the stern frame's cast iron length. The transmitted shock of grounding had also forced the rudder vertically upwards, its stock smashing through the steering compartment deck. Chapelon's systematic destruction had started the moment her stern had swung into Hadston Carrs.

As Chapelon's master opened the starboard wheelhouse door again, almost like a well scripted drama, the near-by coast sprang into instant life. One after another, powerful searchlights suddenly illuminated and focussed their beams onto his crippled ship. Other lights flooded their lumens across a piece of elevated ground. They also reflected off a furious and potentially lethal surf line that blocked his ship's crew from the safety of the so tantalisingly close, but for them, impossibly distant dry land. It was there that their only chance of survival lay. Lifting his binoculars, he watched figures hunched and bent double against the wind, at times physically grabbing tufts of grass in order to drag themselves and equipment into position. One of them would be his French voice who had encouraged them from the start. He briefly wondered who the man was and what he was like? He wanted to meet him. It was with a strange and disturbing realisation, as he tried to conceal his own gnawing wish to survive from his anxious crew that he concluded it was not so much the thought of never seeing his own admittedly remote family again, or even fear of how he might die. He was simply desperate to meet that coastguard, whose name he did not even know, so he could shake the man's hand.

"Mayday, Tyne-Tees Coastguard, Tyne-Tees Charlie."

Roy was keeping his radio procedure extremely tight now he was permanently on Channel Sixteen.

"Chapelon has grounded, repeat, Chapelon has grounded. Bows pointing south, stern on Hadston Carrs. Preparing to commence rescue by Breeches Buoy."

"Mayday, Tyne-Tees Charlie, Tyne-Tees Coastguard, copied." Blyth auxiliary-in-charge joined Roy.

It was a good location to observe the erection of the rocket launcher and see the cripple just beyond the surf.

"How long?" shouted Roy to him, as close by, all of Amble's and Craster's coast rescue teams fought their own battle against the elements to erect and secure the Eighty-Three Millimetre rocket launcher.

"Less than Five Minutes!" he bellowed back, in a voice that had no need of a loud hailer.

"Mayday, Chapelon, Tyne Tees Charlie, Interco Golf Tango, je Repeter, Interco Golf Tango."

Using the International Codes again, Roy was telling them they were about to commence their rescue by Breaches Buoy.

It was Chapelon's third officer who responded to the radio call that had suddenly seemed to fill the wheelhouse with sound. Her master nodded to the chief officer as confirmation they were to start putting their own pre-agreed plan into effect. Crew members clad in life-jackets and foul weather gear filed out across two decks on the starboard side, ready to catch the rocket line that was about to be fired.

Atop their chosen dune, a dozen men struggled to hold the rocket launcher in position as their colleagues hammered foot-long, solo cliff rescue stakes into thick vegetation and secured lashings to the base of the launcher's legs. Three men had to manipulate each of the two tall, front legs. Blyth's deputy auxiliary in charge and two other men unwound a length of heavy-duty cable as they prepared the rocket's ignition mechanism, giving distance between the launcher and a firing box they had filled with batteries before positioning it behind, to one side of, and downwind of the launcher. Two more men dragged a low, square box, packed with eight-millimetre diameter rocket line into position close to the back of the launcher. More still carried a long, grey, heavy wooden packing case up to the launcher itself. Meanwhile, Blyth's deputy secured a small explosive squib between the electrical contacts on the launcher end of the cable. He raised and lowered his flashlight in the direction of his colleague who was helping him who then pressed the firing box's plunger. The squib popped and flashed. The firing circuit was tested and ready. Willing hands prised the partially loosened lid off the heavy packing case revealing the cylindrical shape of a Schermully eighty-three millimetres rescue rocket, painted in pale grey, with black stencilled information on its side. A light U-shaped stirrup frame, wrapped around the rocket's flat nose that extended beyond its rear formed a bridle with a wire trace. The wire, close to the rocket's exhaust efflux, protected the vital cordage of the rescue line from hot gasses that would have otherwise burnt it through when the rocket towed it out to the ship. The missile's interior was packed with plastic explosives as a propellant. A length of cable with a connector emerged from the choked efflux at its rear. Against the furious elements, it took the full strength of four, struggling men to lift the rocket and slide it into the launcher. Blyth's deputy, lying on his back, close to the rear of the launcher tied the rocket line end to the wire trace and then connected the two cables that completed the firing circuit. Everybody moved clear of the launcher, well behind Craster's auxiliary in charge who now held the firing box. A torch was carefully raised and lowered in the direction of Blyth auxiliary in charge. All was ready.

"Wait," commanded Roy to his colleague, lifting his hand portable radio to his lips. "Mayday, Chapelon, Interco Golf Tango Un," he declared.

"Oui, Golf Tango Un."

Chapelon instantly understood the code meaning, 'I am about to fire a rocket.'

Roy immediately turned to give his auxiliary in charge colleague the thumbs up.

Blyth started raising and lowering his powerful torch in the direction of his Craster colleague with the firing box…

The response was dramatic and instant. A streak of orange flame leapt out from the rear of the rocket as it raced from its launcher. Its attached line ripped out of its box as the rocket's continuous, blasting roar seemed to overpower the enormity of the storm itself. The trailing line, rising from its box was suddenly caught by a frightful wind gust, that jerked the towing rocket into an instant, vertical trajectory. The rocket continued on its now uncontrolled path, curling through a full one hundred and eighty degrees, whilst dragging what was now a lethal tangle behind it as it suddenly dove into the waiting rescue teams.

Men shouted hurried, frightened warnings, before scattering and flattening themselves into the sand and scrub. It wasn't just the rocket tearing over their heads that alarmed them.

The real danger was its flailing line that was capable of dragging a man to his death. As the rocket's impetus finally expired, its line fell limp and harmless, among the cursing, bedraggled and chaotic bodies of the auxiliary teams.

Roy picked himself up, spitting sand from where he had tried to bury himself in the dunes.

"Mayday, Chapelon, Tyne-Tees Charlie."

He simply asked them to wait.

Chapelon's master almost seemed to grunt a reply as he stared intently through his binoculars. His stomach felt hollow. Another failure. Then to his astonishment, having witnessed what was literally an explosive assault on the men who were there to help them, he watched the people ashore pick themselves up, shake themselves down and continue to almost casually go about the business of trying to get his crew off his ship.

"*C'est pas tres bien,*" announced Roy blandly, in what was a powerful understatement. "Interco Golf Tango encore."

The master managed a brief smile. After the frightening and dramatic scene, he had just witnessed, the assault on the assembled coastguards by their own rocket seemed to be being written off as a minor inconvenience. Their stubborn refusal to accept failure was evident yet again. *But,* he wondered, *How many rockets were there left to fire?*

Back on the shore-line and amongst the dunes, the reality for the rescue crews was that they had been badly shaken. Dusting themselves off, there were the first signs of resigned weariness as they prepared once again for another attempt to get a line out to the ship.

The driving rain, wind and spray, the blasting sand and the near deafening noise were all taking their toll on peoples' senses and resilience. Hunched almost double, the district controller seemed to crab over to Blyth auxiliary in charge.

Gripping his shoulder hard, the DC bellowed into his ear, "Use a MoD rocket! An eighteen pounder!"

"That's what I intended to do!" roared back the auxiliary in charge, his temper fraying at the DC stating the obvious, while he returning the favour of being shouted at, to add to his half deafness.

"Mayday, Tyne-Tess Coastguard, Tyne-Tees Charlie."

Roy held his hand-portable radio close to his lips.

Responding to his colleague's acknowledgement from the operations room, he continued, "An attempt to connect with the ship using a Schermully rescue rocket has failed. The elements blew the rocket off course."

There was no need to embellish the brief terror it had caused as it dove into and scattered the coast rescue teams. Nobody had been hurt.

Having also just witnessed the spat between the district controller and his auxiliary in charge, the ops room detected his slight chuckle as he continued, "On the DC's instructions, we are now loading an eighteen pounder!"

"Mayday, Charlie, Tyne-tees copied."

The reply was bland and objective, exactly as it should be, but in the warmth of the MRSC where the pounding generator kept the communications going, the lights burning and the kettle boiling, Roy's colleagues smiled. They guessed correctly what had happened.

At the equipment dump cold hands grabbed a stout, drab, matte-brown, long, wooden packing case, stencilled with bright yellow letters. The military had their own time-honoured way of marking containers containing explosives. Soft, rope-hemp handles had been thoughtfully placed around the stout, heavy, box to help with its carriage.

Compared to its more modern Schermully counterpart that had just disgraced itself so dramatically, the ministry of defence rescue rocket, more commonly known as the Eighteen Pounder for obvious descriptive reasons, was a very different projectile. An adapted anti-tank missile motor; this particular rocket was over thirty years old and packed with a carefully formulated, but now ageing flash-less cordite. It could throw a massive punch. Its age and occasional unpredictability had encouraged the initial choice of a more modern, supposedly reliable, plastic explosives filled projectile by the rescue teams. Men now carried the MoD rocket to the launcher warily as their other colleagues kept a respectable distance. Amble's deputy auxiliary in charge prised off the box's already loosened lid with a crowbar causing those near-by to wince. Nestled inside was a substantial steel tube, painted and stencilled in the same colours as its box. In a separate compartment in the box's front was the rocket's nose cone. It had been deliberately made detachable for safe storage. In theory, should the rocket's cordite ignite spontaneously, then the charge would burn fiercely out of both ends. There was a very real risk of a major conflagration, but a minimal threat of an out-of-control missile causing devastation. That was the theory. Nobody in Tyne-Tees District had ever wished to prove or disprove its principle.

Before the rocket was even loaded into its launcher, the firing circuit was tested with another squib.

Two more team members reluctantly volunteered their additional help to lift the Eighteen Pounder out of its case and hold it steady as the blunt nose-cone was screwed home. Amble's deputy felt for a pair of lugs clicking into position as proof that the nose-cone had been correctly secured. Aided by others, the men struggled against the wind, determined not to drop their cordite filled beast as it slid home into the launcher.

With the rocket properly settled, people breathed more easily and retreated rapidly.

A fresh box of rocket line was positioned behind the launcher and its protruding rear end was fastened to the twin tails on the appropriately named tail block through which the endless whip that would propel the breeches buoy ran. On the block's arse was a stout swivel, to which was attached the jackstay, along which the breaches buoy itself would travel. All the cordage was modern, made of strong braided nylon. To avoid any confusion, the whips were coloured blue, the jackstay red. Skilled hands had tied, or more correctly 'bent', given the nautical nature of the job the rocket line onto the whip tails with a series of spaced hitches. When the tail block was hauled out to the ship, the tails, so vital for securing it to the ship's structure, would fall naturally to hand. A multi-lingual placard hanging from the block was carefully checked. It gave basic instructions in three languages, including French, for when the tackle arrived on the ship.

A heavy length of manila rope was dragged out to the rocket launcher and clipped onto the patiently waiting MoD rescue rocket via a wire trace. The front of the rocket line was secured to its other end. The rope was there to act as a cushion; a shock absorbing spring. The massive initial impetus of the Eighteen Pounder when it was fired would have otherwise snapped the for now carefully stowed line it would then pull out to Chapelon.

People visibly moved even further out of the way as Blyth's deputy made the final connection between rocket and firing cable, before retiring the cable's full length and hiding with the firing box behind a sand hummock.

“We’re ready.” Blyth auxiliary in charge said simply to Roy.

“Mayday, Chapelon, Tyne Tees Charlie, Golf Tango un, je repet, Golf Tango un.”

The reply from the ship was brief and positive.

“Tyne Tees Coastguard, copied.”

His ops room colleagues, as usual, were right on the ball.

Roy nodded at Blyth’s deputy. The firing plunger was pressed and the flash-less cordite ‘flashed’, displaying a blinding yellow flame with an accompanying deafening, explosive blast. The rocket literally leapt from its launcher, throwing the structure askew as it went, slamming into, competing with and defeating the fury of the storm. For a full half second, the cordite swamped the area with its fierce, brilliant yellow light and continuous, overwhelming explosion that became almost unbearable on eardrums. If the Schermully rocket was impressive, this eclipsed all as it raced across the water towards Chapelon. A projectile that was originally intended to punch holes in armour plate, but whose purpose was now a life saver. The massive force of the burning cordite caused the rocket line to rise vertically from its box, as if it were some grotesque Indian Rope Trick, before being dragged by the now dead weight of the Eighteen Pounder in an arc towards the distressed ship.

On board Chapelon, her crew were briefly stunned and shocked by the sudden, brilliant, explosive flash, before they too were assaulted by its continuous, concussive, blast, that tore against the wind and thudded into their ears moments later. Back lit by the shore’s searchlights, they followed the rocket’s ballistic trajectory as it swept right over their stricken ship and dropped into the sea beyond. The line neatly fell over the after end of Chapelon's accommodation where one of the mate's team quickly and eagerly took it in hand. Their vital contact with the shore had been accomplished. As the mate's crew carefully passed the line outboard of obstructions and reached the bridge, the third officer appeared on the starboard bridge wing with their signal lamp, aimed it towards the shore and gently and purposely raised and lowered its penetrating beam. Blyth auxiliary in charge raised his powerful torch in response. Roy acknowledged the visual signal with his radio.

"Break-break, Tyne-Tees Coastguard, we have physical contact with Chapelon, she has retrieved the second line we fired."

"Mayday, Charlie, roger. Tyne Tees standing by."

Once again the massed rescue teams emerged from what shelter they had found, laden with their equipment. The rocket launcher, now looking dejected, askew and scorched black from exhaust gasses and flame, was ruthlessly removed and returned to the dump. Its vital job was done and it was now nothing more than a dangerous obstruction, hindering the work in hand. Its stakes and their lashings were however saved for using elsewhere. A specialist tripod was dragged forward, brought up from the dump by an entourage of struggling people who laid it on the ground, slightly in front of where the rocket launcher had been. Its forward-facing leg had been painted white for easy recognition and deployment, when it was raised to take the jackstay. Well in front of – and on either side of the tripod; long, heavy stakes were driven into the ground with sledge hammers. They would provide anchors for the tethers worn by breast rope men, who would be the first to handle rescued crew as they were brought ashore. The jackstay line box was joined on either side by boxes containing the two halves of the endless whip. All were carefully adjusted, ready for their cordage to be run out to Chapelon. The jackstay's fastenings were double-checked, where it was secured to the arse of the tail block. The endless whip was then threaded through the tail block and the two ends joined by metal clips spliced into the cordage. It was then briefly run, or more correctly rove through the tail block to make sure it would smoothly shuttle the breeches buoy to and from the stricken ship. Everything was ready.

Back on board there had been a brief conference between Chapelon's master, mate and her bosun to decide where the best place would be to secure the breeches buoy tail block. They quickly settled on a strong point on deck, just aft of the bridge. The protruding deck below the lifeboats could then be used for embarkation into the breeches buoy itself as it hung from its cordage. Those of her remaining crew who were not involved with securing the breeches buoy were all now sheltered, with their feelings of anticipation and adrenaline surging, in the wheelhouse. Their senses were already becoming overwhelmed by the noise that screamed though the now wedged open, starboard sliding door. That open door guaranteed everybody had easy access to the deck below, without the need to enter what was potentially dangerous accommodation. As the ship's frames and plate work distorted and bent, while Chapelon pounded herself to pieces, people could become trapped behind jammed doors and buckled bulkheads.

Several men could now be seen crouching behind the bridge wing dodgers, as they held the vital rocket line, waiting further instructions from the teams ashore.

Still fighting and struggling against the elements, drawing on unknown reserves of energy, the rescue teams continued their preparatory work. Landwards, behind the tripod, two long stakes had been driven through holes in a purpose-made, substantial timber board, taking advantage of firm ground and vegetation within the dunes. The carefully angled stakes now acted as a cleat for securing the jackstay. The front stake had also been thrust through a metal strop. It would take the hook from a luff tackle used for tensioning the jackstay. The breeches buoy was for now sheltering behind a nearby hummock. At first glance everything about the breeches buoy seemed to be old and decaying, belying its hidden strengths. The buoy itself contained a buoyant core of cork, stiffened and protected by stitched canvas, painted in red and white. It could not have differed more markedly with modern, moulded plastic, man-overboard life buoys. To add to its venerable age was the natural fibre cordage that bound and strengthened the buoy and also provided fastenings. The impression of obsoleteness was completed by the stained plain and stiff canvas breeches that hung below the buoy, in these, Chapelon's survivors would sit. One of the rescue team, after filling its container with new batteries, checked a red riding-light that was also thoughtfully attached to the breeches buoy to indicate its progress to those on the shore.

The district controller joined a small huddle formed by Blyth auxiliary in charge and Roy. Their hand portable radios crackled, confirming that all was ready for starting their lifesaving operation. Roy raised his radio to his lips, asking Chapelon to start hauling on the rocket line. At the same time Blyth slowly raised and lowered his lamp in the direction of Chapelon's bridge.

"Mayday, Tyne-Tees Coastguard; Charlie, we are about to deploy the jackstay to Chapelon."

Keeping the operations room briefed was now an automatic protocol for Roy.

"Tyne-Tees copied."

Once again the reply was concise, professional and clipped. On board Chapelon, her master acknowledged the latest communication and her third officer raised and lowered his signal lamp as further affirmation. Behind the bridge wing dodger, several pairs of hands began hauling on the rocket line, as they struggled against the dead-weight of the apparatus being towed from the shore. Chapelon's master, mate and chief engineer continuously observed the illuminated scene on land through binoculars. It was more than mere curiosity. They watched the men working ashore with professional interest as they lifted their assembled cordage high, working the jackstay and whips, to help the crew who were taking the strain on their ship. Nobody on board had ever conceived they would be participants in an event quite like this. The master scanned the straining figures beyond the surf, most of them clad in dark oilskins and Weather Guards, as their struggle was more against the weather than the job in-hand, wondering if he had inadvertently spotted his personal coastguard, who was somewhere out there amongst the struggling people, waiting to meet them. Hauling the rocket line became easier as the tail block got ever closer to Chapelon. Even though its overall weight increased as the jackstay and whips snaked towards them, the force on the line they were hauling decreased. It was simple mathematics. The crew understood instinctively. After all, they were used to operating derricks in union purchase rig when they worked cargo. The strain on derrick runner lines as their angles widened under a lifting load, increased massively. Now they could sense the parallelogram of forces through their own hands as the tail block inched its way towards them. The bosun suddenly felt, rather than saw the tails as they fell naturally to hand. He briefly smiled in approval at the way they had been bent onto the rocket line. Even though the equipment was land-based, largely operated by volunteers from all walks of life; efficient and safe operation of the breeches buoy demanded the highest standards of seamanship.

Back on the shore, Blyth auxiliary in charge had moved to their main working area atop the firm dune, megaphone in hand. As the jackstay and whips followed the tail block out to the ship, their cordage needed careful management. The whips in particular, had to be kept reasonably close together, but not so close as to become tangled. From the three boxes out of which the ropes emerged, men maintained a light, but positive tension. He then almost inadvertently noticed that another person he didn't recognise and clearly from another Coast rescue Company had dedicated himself to monitoring and maintaining their lighting. His was a never-ending, monotonous, almost thankless task of constantly patrolling and adjusting. The paraffin pressure lamps in particular needed to have their fuel tanks regularly pumped up, to keep their mantles burning bright and white. He felt his heart lift at the sight. True teamwork from men, many of whom were not used to working together; but all were thinking ahead and on their feet.

The district controller too made ready to move to a better location for maintaining his overall tactical control. Roy ducked out of the wind, briefly removing his goggles as he rubbed sudden weariness from his eyes, before speaking to his boss in the quieter lee side of their dune.

"I'd like to go behind the breast rope men to where Chapelon's crew will disembark. I can then speak to each one and help maintain a running tote of her survivors. They can then be directed towards the WRVS truck and police."

The DC quickly saw the sense in the idea. "Yes," he agreed. "I'll have Blyth AIC arrange men as escorts to see them safely out of the way. You know you can't physically record anything in this, it would be impossible."

"No need to," responded his colleague, "we know there are forty-one men on that ship. I can ask each one how many are left as we retrieve them and then relay the information to the ops room with my radio. As far as I know, at least the operations rooms are still warm and dry," he added with just a hint or irony.

The district controller lightly touched Roy's shoulder.

"Good man," he said. "I'll try to ensure your work out here does not go unrewarded or unrecognised."

"Thank you," responded Roy with genuine feeling, as he pulled his goggles back over his eyes. "At the end of the day I'm still just part of a team."

The DC nodded, smiling at the reply, as he moved off towards Blyth auxiliary in charge.

Back on board Chapelon, the bosun and two seamen finished securing the block's tails across the base of a stanchion, their selected hard point. He also managed to splice a length of rope he produced from his pocket around the eye at the end of the tail block's swivel to which the tails were attached and lash that home onto a near-by ringbolt, an insurance policy to back up the tails. The bosun too was an expert seaman and wanted his own belts and braces! As the bosun approached the near-by bridge wing he saw the third mate raise the signal lamp, directing it towards the shore in a vertical motion, a visual confirmation that the tail block was fast.

Roy did not hesitate with his radio calling Chapelon, confirming their visual signal had been received, before asking the ship to wait a few minutes while they prepared the 'Pantalon de Souvetage' – the Breeches Buoy.

"Tyne-Tees Coastguard, Charlie," he continued without taking a breath, "Tail block is secure on Chapelon, stand by for deployment of Breeches Buoy."

Raising his radio to his lips again, a sudden thought struck him. The placard on the tail block included instructions to sit deep in the buoy's breeches. These instructions were also stencilled in English on the red and white painted buoy itself. When the breeches unyielding crotch piece impacted with somebody's groin, there was a strong temptation to automatically raise oneself against the discomfort. He felt he needed to reinforce that advice, adding that the rider should also keep looking at the lights ashore, not at the sea below, or turn to see his ship.

Chapelon's master almost seemed to grunt a reply again. His mind briefly wondered about what sort of training these people underwent? Battling against a ferocious storm and consumed with their immediate task of hard, physical rescue, they still seemed to be thinking of every last little detail that could be of immense importance to his people.

Blyth auxiliary in charge had now donned his own protective cliff goggles as he set about directing the final preparations for deploying the breeches buoy. Roy stood back with the district controller, observing. This was now the teams' show and theirs alone.

Their own routines had been thoroughly drilled into them. They had no need for outside interference. It would have been both superfluous and unappreciated. Men dragged and carried the whip boxes, clawing against the constant wind that battered them, until they were well apart. Others constantly pulled and worked the whips to ensure they remained running freely through the tail block out on Chapelon. Once in position, they tipped the remaining whip lines out of their boxes and neatened them on the ground. Two men carried the whips' free ends and brought them together, before joining their metal clips.

The whips were now endless; a continuous loop. The luff tackle, whose reeves had been neatly platted for stowage and transport was unravelled. The block that included a set of long tails was pointed towards Chapelon. The block at the other end, that culminated in a hook, was attached to the strop previously fitted to the forward stake of the cleat. Eight men hauled hard on the red jackstay, pulling-in as much slack as they could, struggling to stay upright, not only against the wind, but also against Chapelon, whose erratic movement on the rocks was now being transmitted to them through the jackstay line.

A bight of the jackstay was placed around the cleat.

"Up Tripod!" commanded Blyth auxiliary in charge.

Six men moved forward and swung the white painted leg until it was pointing directly at the wreck on the rocks. In a concerted effort, they then raised the tripod and drove its pointed leg ends hard into the ground. The stakes and lashings that had been recovered from the rocket launcher were now hammered home by each tripod leg and lashed tight, providing additional stability. A snatch block was produced and shackled into its fastening, so it hung beneath the tripod top. One of the men produced a marlin spike and twisted the shackle's pin tight. He then 'moused' the pin against the shackle's bow with a thin length of wire that he carefully twisted, ensuring it could not work free. Finally, he opened the cheek on the block, ready to receive the jackstay, giving it valuable elevation for when they started running the breaches buoy.

Blyth auxiliary in charge was gesturing with his arms for the jackstay to be secured in the snatch block. Those tending the cleat slackened the line a little – and as Chapelon rolled towards them, it provided a little more line. This enabled the tripod erectors to quickly lift the jackstay and slide it into the block. The snatch cheek was slammed home and secured with a stout split pin.

"Dog the tails!" Blyth's deputy auxiliary in charge had anticipated the next command and moved to the block on the fore part of the luff tackle.

Four members from the Amble team took the luff's hauling part in hand and waited…the deputy turned his back to the wind and started platting the block's tails around the jackstay, left hand over right hand, left over right…when he got to the end of the tails, he tied them off with short bits of cord. The end result could have passed as expert art work in any hairdressing salon. He smartly moved clear of the dogged jackstay, ready for the Amble team to tension it. The platted tails were now an effective stopper for the luff tackle to work on. Blyth's AIC quickly scanned the jackstay, ensuring all was clear, before nodding to the Amble boys. The turn around the cleat had already been cast off. Now they applied full tension to the jackstay through the mechanical advantage of the luff tackle.

A problem occurred immediately. Chapelon was still rolling and grinding herself to pieces on Hadston Carrs. The jackstay was subject to all of her death throes, transferring her movements to the men hauling on the luff tackle. They struggled, but finally managed to bring the jackstay to its correct tension.

"Nipper the Luff!" roared Blyth.

Three more men from the Tynemouth Volunteer Life Brigade moved forwards, gripping the parts of the luff tackle that lay between its blocks, effectively jamming the luff tackle tight. The Amble men started to turn the luff's free end around the cleat. Chapelon suddenly lurched to seaward, away from them. The jackstay strained dangerously as the Volunteer Life Brigade men released and rapidly stepped back from the luff tackle. Amble's men threw the turns off the cleat as line squealed through the luff's blocks. It had been close, but the jackstay had been saved from snapping. Amble's auxiliary in charge had been quietly observing the whole episode. They simply couldn't turn the luff's free end up on the cleat, the jackstay was likely to part under excessive tension! Yet maintaining the correct tightness on the jackstay, particularly when men were riding the breaches buoy was absolutely essential. He ran in a crab-like crouch over to his colleague in arms from Blyth.

"I'll get my lads to keep the jackstay under tension by taking the luff in hand. Can you and your team help?" he asked, turning to the three Tynemouth men, who grinned and nodded in response. “That gives me sixteen hands or more,” he continued. “We can bend an extra length of line onto the luff and give ourselves plenty of space to haul.”

Blyth agreed to the plan without hesitation. There was probably no other option. Exposed to the fury of the elements atop the dunes, Amble had committed his men and others to a tedious, monotonous but vital task that would make massive demands on their stamina, strength and determination. The team tied their additional cordage onto the free end of the luff's hauling line and took up position along it. They immediately hauled on the jackstay, tightening the essential link to Chapelon to its correct tension. Then, almost like automatons, started to walk backwards and forwards, luff in hand, moving in unison with Chapelon as she continued her self-destruction on the near-by rocks. A potential show-stopper had been solved; the rescue continued.

With his goggles secured tightly around his eyes, Blyth auxiliary in charge turned and faced directly into the wind. Blowing sand and spume smashed painfully into his face, but he had to decide on the wind's precise direction. That would determine which whip they would secure the breeches buoy to. The storm, well in excess of hurricane force was hitting them almost head-on. For nearly a minute, he maintained his painful posture, periodically dropping his head, so that he could at least breathe, gulping at the tortured air. It had been difficult, testing his knowledge and judgement to its limits, but now he knew which whip to use. He turned and found men from the Boulmer team waiting patiently behind him with the breeches buoy.

“Right Hand Whip!” he shouted, pointing to the blue line that lay to their right. “Attach with ‘B’ method.”

The Boulmer boys moved forwards, next to the tripod and grabbed a length of the whip that lay to its right. They attached the whip fore and aft on to lines that formed part of the breeches buoy's cordage. The loose end of the whip that formed a hanging loop, was gathered up and neatly packed beneath a toggle thoughtfully placed on the side of the breaches buoy. That would prevent it snagging obstructions on the shore, the sea bed or on Chapelon herself. Next, they attached a smallish snatch-block, the buoys traveller, onto the landwards end of the buoy's cordage and as they felt a brief lull in the wind, raised the specialist buoy and presented the traveller block to the jackstay in front of the tripod, slamming its cheek shut without ceremony and securing it. As a final act, they switched on the buoy's red riding light.

Blyth was given the thumbs up, followed by a torch pointed towards him being raised and lowered, the 'affirmative' signal.

His breast rope men were ready, wrapped in layers of clothes, their faces swathed in scarves and their goggles pulled tight over their eyes. Around their chests they wore heavy, blue canvas harnesses that were reinforced with small steel bars. They moved forward and attached their tethers to the two stakes. Blyth had delayed deploying these men for as long as he dared. They would be in the most exposed position of all, subject to everything the weather could throw at them. With the sea crashing and breaking in dangerous proximity, they double checked their lengths of safety line.

"Are we ready?" asked Roy. Blyth nodded.

He spoke in French, keeping his words short and clipped.

"Mayday, Chapelon Tyne-Tees Charlie."

He told the ship to prepare their first evacuee for the breeches buoy, deliberately keeping his tone both neutral and emotionless. The same voice he used for broadcasting the weather in the operations room.

Blyth raised his loud hailer to his lips with renewed purpose.

"Man the left whip!"

Available manpower from every company between The Tyne and The Tweed reacted, trying to ignore the blasting discomforts and dangers of the elements as they took up positions on the blue, snaking line to his left. Two men tended the right-hand whip pile, ready to guide its cordage on its journey out to Chapelon, behind the breeches buoy.

Snags and tangles were now unthinkable. Roy had been observing carefully and now called the operations room.

"Mayday, Tyne-Tees Coastguard; Charlie. The buoy is transiting to Chapelon. Will advise when the first survivor is ashore and update the tote."

Feeling their own adrenaline rising, the operations room quickly gave a routine acknowledgment leaving the frequency free for communications exchanges at the site.

On board Chapelon, they waited tensely and with mounting anticipation. Their first trip cadet was the first nominee for sending ashore. The master gave him a package to take with him, as the nervous teenager tucked it beneath his bulky, orange lifejacket and made his way down to the boat deck; already soaked through, despite his heavy, protective clothing. At the point of embarkation, he listened with mounting fear as the tail block squeaked above his head and the red light marking the breeches buoy's progress along the jackstay, steadily became brighter. The mate, supervising the evacuation gave him a final briefing; surprisingly soft and gentle, given the tone he usually used with his cadets. He finished with a smile and words of encouragement as he reminded his cadet to keep looking at the shore and the lights out there, and to sit low in the breeches, regardless of any discomfort!

The breeches buoy suddenly, almost unexpectedly arrived; its traveller block banging against the tail block immediately above their heads. The third mate, observing from the bridge wing raised and lowered his signal lamp and received a similar response from the shore. The mate and bosun pulled the buoy down to deck level and invited the cadet to get in. He was looking at the old buoy in astonishment. To say it appeared time expired was an understatement! He had never seen a hand-painted, canvas coated, cork lifebuoy before, whose cordage looked suspiciously ancient. By choice he would have left well alone. That was not an option as he stood over the buoy, one foot in each hole made by the collapsed breeches on Chapelon's deck. The bosun's tones and gestures were far from friendly as he hurried him into position. The cadet felt the wet, stiff and stained canvas breeches as the buoy was pulled up around him and he held onto cordage around its edge. There was a token of padding for his crotch that would no doubt support his full weight, but comfort with this device was an obvious afterthought, given the sparsity of the padding. He guessed the journey would be both fearful and painful! Unseen by him, the third mate raised and lowered his signal lamp. The tail block briefly creaked and suddenly, he was being swept off the ship and left hanging in the breeches, grimacing in discomfort and pain, but remembering his instructions. Close to his head, the traveller block rasped its way along the jackstay, showering a spray of water into his face. The wind buffeted and roared on his back. He remembered to keep low in the buoy, watching the approaching lights with watering eyes and trying to ignore the crazy, violent world around him, where waves and breaking surf crashed against his suspended legs, whilst he held on to the buoy and a thoughtfully provided steadying line, for dear life. The jackstay seemed to swing and bounce, as unseen by the cadet, the Amble team with their extra helpers fought and struggled to maintain its tension. The pull on the whips became smoother, as the combined might of every spare available hand from the Auxiliary Coastguard Service between The Tyne and the Scottish Border provided motive power on the whips, as they hauled by walking as far back as they could in a continuous relay. He was in a crazy, suspended world of blackness, with eye watering brilliant light ahead of him. He instantly became aware of receding surf, driving sand and two figures in front of him, straining like hunting dogs on their leash. It came as a shock when without any warning, the two breast rope men grabbed him and the buoy. He was aware of dry ground under his feet, as with the buoy still around him, they directed him back to the tripod, before dropping the buoy and letting him step out.

As the stunned cadet staggered out of the Breeches Buoy, Roy suddenly gripped him and shouted against the wind. The teenager thought Roy looked a little like the old Breeches Buoy itself, clad in an ancient, battered oilskin bound with string, Sunderland Supporter's hat secured to his head with the band from his goggles. To the cadet's modern eye, he had become trapped in a time warp. Roy bellowed into his ear, asking how many were left on his ship? The cadet was speechless, after the last few shocking hours he had temporarily become totally mute. Roy managed a smile and told him to go with two men for food and a hot drink, before cheerfully welcoming him to England! Two broadly grinning auxiliary coastguards approached the stunned young man, grabbed an arm each and guided him towards sustenance. Unbeknown, the teenager's ordeal was far from over. Acute embarrassment awaited from the generous souls of the good ladies from the WRVS. After observing his frightened youthfulness, they decided to take him under their ample wings and subject him to a good dose of mothering!

"Mayday, Tyne Tees Coastguard. Charlie, first man ashore, forty to go!"

In the operations room, the atmosphere briefly became electric. They were finally winning against the odds, where helicopter and lifeboat had failed. The rescue had started. People smiled, Jack briefly punched his fist into the air. Then it was time to concentrate again. They still had a long way to go. In Druridge Bay, the district controller allowed himself a moment to feel triumphant and smiled briefly as he watched the struggling teams react with a new jauntiness. The arrival of the cadet ashore had worked like a magic elixir. Roy let the ship know their first man was ashore. Her master acknowledged the transmission and shouted the news to all of those around him. The coastguards were finally succeeding against seemingly impossible odds!

Already, the buoy was being run back out to the ship, ready to receive the next evacuee, their mess boy who listened intently to the mate. He repeated the message that the mate wanted him to pass to the coastguards, to let them know there would be thirty-nine men left on board. He nodded with a grin as he made ready for the ride of a lifetime. He gasped as he felt his crotch twinge against his weight as it fell across the canvas breeches, before lurching into the stormy darkness, being propelled towards the blaze of lights that marked the safety of the shore. The breast rope men grabbed the mess boy, before his feet even touched the ground, dragging him and the buoy towards the tripod.

Everybody was smiling as he stepped clear of the breeches. Roy smiled too, telling him he was number two ashore. Without being asked further, the mess boy told him there were thirty-nine souls remaining on board, before pumping his hand with glee and wishing him Merry Christmas! He happily accompanied his escorts to the WRVS van to enjoy a well-earned hot drink and a snack.

Roy spoke into his radio again.

"Mayday, Tyne-Tees Coastguard, Tyne Tees Charlie, we now have two men from Chapelon ashore. Confirming thirty-nine remain on board."

Even as the operations room responded to the radio transmission, repeating the essential information, the Breeches Buoy was nearly halfway along the jackstay, being quickly hauled out to Chapelon to continue recovering her crew from the wreck.

Up on the Starboard Bridge Wing, Chapelon's master, binoculars clamped to his eyes had managed to identify his special coastguard among all the other huddled figures moving around on the shore. He studied the goggle clad, ragged figure, sporting a ridiculous red and white hat, as he questioned their mess boy. His attire seemed somehow appropriate, given the way he was speaking their native language! The master could not help chuckling. Roy's layer of outer clothes, cobbled hurriedly together for the elements, facing a situation he had never anticipated when he appeared on watch in the operations room, seemed to match his willingness to improvise, as he had constantly struggled to find a way to win through. Shake his hand? If the master survived and made it to the shore, he would willingly hug him.

The Breeches Buoy's traveller block clunked against the tail block on Chapelon. The next evacuee had already received his final instructions from the mate. The third mate worked his signal lamp and as the momentum of the operation increased as the struggling crews adapted to the changing situation. The next man was rapidly on his way to the safety of the shore.

In Druridge Bay, team members swapped to form fresh relays, relieving each other on the whips. It was cracking muscles and the sheer physical endurance of dedicated people, many of whom were close to pension age that was driving this dramatic rescue. The Amble and Tynemouth men remained on the luff, working the jackstay, gauging movement, as the lurching and rolling of Chapelon became more erratic and pronounced while she continued to tear herself apart. But her keel held, her back remained unbroken, buying her crew vital time as they were swept off their ship to safety with equipment that seemed as ancient as the sea itself. On the shore, hands became red raw as they were chaffed by working the wet cordage, soaked with the sea, whose salt formed an added abrasive against their frozen flesh.

About a third of Chapelon's crew had been brought ashore, when her lights flickered dramatically and then continued to burn steadily. The engine room beneath them had finally succumbed to the intrusive sea and was flooding, stopping her main generators and ruining their switch boards. The emergency generator behind the bridge now had to cope with the load on its own. It's exhaust growl deepened as it threw out more amps to keep Chapelon's vital illuminations burning, providing brightness, safety and comfort. The sickly-sweet pungency of heavy fuel oil drifted up to assail the crews' nostrils from the sea as her double bottom fuel tanks ruptured. The chief engineer grabbed his second and the two men moved aft, to check all was well with the last, desperate source of electricity on their stricken ship.

Just over half an hour later, the twenty first man was in the breaches buoy. Half the crew were now safely ashore. An ambulance had arrived on scene, released from other demands the awful weather had placed on the emergency services. People living nearby and devoid of power, had opened their homes, willingly providing warmth and shelter for the survivors, along with additional supplies of food and water to replenish those brought by the good ladies of the WRVS, who freely and happily ladled out hot tea, coffee, soup, sandwiches and sausage rolls to those who were simply glad to be alive. The ambulance crew for now, dealt with nothing more serious than cuts and bruises among the evacuees and increasingly among the hard-worked coast rescue personnel too. The police were desperately attempting to collect names with little success. Their own Northumbrian dialect, matched against guttural, accented, French was having little impact. All around, many people volunteered their help, willing to assist in any way they could, but the main task and burden remained with the skilled rescue teams, as they dug deep into their own reserves, manhandling the entire crew off a ship. They would have gladly partaken of rest, tea, coffee, snacks and relief from the elements, but they simply had no time. Everybody was now aware of the stench of heavy fuel oil, blasting in on the wind. Their time was running out.

On board Chapelon, a little drama was being played out between her master, mate and chief engineer. Of her three great men, the mate had started it, mainly as a distraction for her crew who still awaited rescue, demanding he should be the last to leave their ship. The chief then interceded and insisted that privilege was his. He strongly argued that as it was all the main engine's fault, it was his responsibility and his call!

Between the three of them he also understood the emergency generator and he was the only single man among them! Her master had none of it. Chapelon was his ship, it was his right and duty to be last off and his was the final word! He had already prepared essential ship's papers and a crew list that were waiting in the wheelhouse in a substantial leather bag with a shoulder strap for taking with him. The other two still dramatically objected; but the master remained steadfast. His was the rule of law, even on a ship that was becoming a wreck! The chief engineer then noisily pulled rank on the mate, insisting he would be the penultimate evacuee. The master agreed to the chief's request and earned a mouthful of abuse from the mate for not supporting him.

The spat between Chapelon's three great men had worked. It brought a little light relief and some much-needed entertainment to the remaining people around them.

Meanwhile, In the abyss between them and the shore, the Breeches Buoy continued its life-saving shuttle.

Then suddenly, almost unexpectedly, the third mate found it was his turn to leave.

Those remaining on board could now be counted on two hands. He passed the bridge signal lamp to his colleague the second mate, who would ride the breeches buoy after the third engineer and radio officer. The master briefly stopped his young deck officer and offered his thanks. The third mate had always impressed him. During the last few hours his capabilities and steady nature had been tested and well and truly proven. The master watched him climb into the Breeches Buoy, sensibly and without fuss, before starting his swinging, jolting journey towards the shore. When the third mate identified himself to Roy, he saw him smile. It meant their work on this dangerous, wind-swept beach would soon be over. Roy guessed correctly his rescue team colleagues would be glad of the break and some sustenance. Nobody could deny them that. They had more than earned it.

Then, in seemingly little time, it was the second mate's turn. He handed the signal lamp to the mate, who carried the lamp and its portable battery down to their embarkation point. The master collected his shoulder bag from the wheelhouse, feeling his ship prepare for her final death throes. It couldn't be long now, as she continued to grate and flex beneath his feet. His emotions had been carefully kept in check, but were now bursting outwards as he suddenly felt for Chapelon. Even in her final hours, she had held herself together, literally buying her crew time to get safely ashore. She had been a good ship and was now suffering an ungracious and undignified end. When the master joined his colleagues at embarkation, the breeches buoy had already returned, ready for the second engineer and his dramatic appendix scar. Beneath his lifejacket and a strong, warm coat, he was still clad in overalls and working boots.

As the second engineer arrived on the beach, still naturally sullen with the news that only three remained on board, Roy quietly reflected they might just succeed in getting all of Chapelon's crew ashore without them suffering major injuries or fatalities. By any standard, the collective performance of the coast rescue companies had been outstanding. He saw the district controller looking in his direction and lifted three frozen fingers. The DC nodded and waited, hoping above all hope they would pull this one off successfully. Heaven alone knew, every person in his district deserved a share in the triumph.

After the mate arrived, still furious that the 'Old Man' would not let him go last, the chief engineer arrived ashore in the Breeches Buoy, wearing his carpet slippers. As he stepped out, assisted by astonished breast rope men, he held his hand up to Roy to stop him and felt in a pocket for his battered old spectacles, held together with fuse wire and Araldite. He carefully settled them on the bridge of his nose, before offering his right hand in greeting. Roy burst into laughter, confirming with the chief engineer he was the fortieth crew member to be rescued.

The chief then confirmed that only the master remained on board.

Roy suddenly felt light headed, warmly welcoming the chief and pointing towards the WRVS station as he gestured into the dunes. Without hesitation the chief engineer started to waddle off in the general direction, before his escorts had been able to reach him.

One man left; the ship's master. In the operations room, the tension could be cut with a knife. Could they? Would they pull this one off?

Chapelon's master looked around at his now deserted ship, whose lights continued to burn faithfully. She was in a bad way. After all of this, including the inevitable inquiry into her loss, might she be his last command? He felt a twinge of sadness for Chapelon. She really didn't deserve to die like this, a once elegant ship, grinding herself to pieces and spewing out her cargo on a storm swept beach in Northern England.

It was the Breeches Buoy banging against the tail block that shook him out of his reverie. He raised the signal lamp to let the shore know and then tossed it into the buoy. He then had to struggle to get into the Breaches Buoy itself without anybody to help him. *The loneliness of command,* he reflected. Finally, he managed to settle in the stiff canvas breeches. He pulled the trigger on the signal lamp and directed it towards the shore, gently raising and lowering its beam. Immediately, tension came on the whips and he felt himself being hoisted into the air, the impact of the crotch piece semi-winding him. He tossed the signal lamp down on Chapelon's deck, where its glass shattered. And then, with seemingly undue haste he was being dragged into the night, looking ahead all the time despite the temptation to look back at his shattered command.

He quickly felt the full ferocity of the storm on his back. Beyond her immediacy, Chapelon offered no lee. The buffeting was continuous, the noise almost overwhelmed his senses. Immediately ahead of him, the traveller block grated against the jackstay as tension was maintained on the right whip, dragging him towards the shore. His cap, that he had remembered to jam tight on his head, went whirling into the sea. Breaking wave tops pummelled his legs, while the rough old, soaking wet canvas breeches battered his calves. Midway, the buoy seemed to dip alarmingly as the Amble team, with their extra help from Tynemouth Volunteer Life Brigade, all willing, but now tired with bleeding hands, continued to struggle against both Chapelon and the elements as they fought to maintain tension on the gyrating jackstay. The Breeches Buoy started to rise. Chapelon's master forcibly had to ignore his continuing discomfort and screwed his eyes against the increasing intensity of light being directed towards him. The temptation was to raise an arm as shade and to lose a vital handhold. The figures of the two breast rope men, at first almost ghostly, suddenly came into focus, still straining on their leashes, reaching out to take hold of both him and the Breeches Buoy. A hand suddenly gripped the cordage at the front of the Breeches Buoy, reaching up for the traveller block, to prevent it striking his head. The other man gripped the master's jacket, springing one of its buttons and held onto the side of the buoy. He felt solid land under his feet as they walked both buoy and contents towards the tripod. The Breeches Buoy was allowed to fall to the ground as tension was removed from its red jackstay. Ahead of the master stood his coastguard.

Goggles scratched and grazed from sand and debris, the skin of his face battered red raw from the elements, Macham hat in place and jauntily showing off its Sunderland colours. Close inspection showed his scarf to be a torn-off section of roller towel, while the orange length of rocket line that held his oilskin together remained firm.

"Bonjour, Commodore," Roy joyfully shouted, *"vous avais Nombre Quarante et un, combien les autres hommes sur Chapelon?"*

"Rien!" responded the master suddenly laughing and shouting, "Rien!" – none.

He moved to grasp his coastguard, but he faced a raised a hand as Roy reached for his hand portable radio that had been dangling on its strap. With fingers numb with cold, he raised it to his lips and pressed the transmit button.

"Mayday, Tyne Tees coastguard, this is Tyne Tees Charlie. All crew have been recovered from Chapelon, I repeat, all her crew are safely ashore. Cancel distress, I say again, cancel distress."

After all that had happened, Roy felt that his final transmission was appropriate and possibly well deserved, even if it broke protocol a little. It was now up to the operations room to compose and formulate the broadcast with the pro-words 'Silonce Finee' that would formally cancel the distress priority and re-establish normal working on VHF Channel Sixteen.

"Reverting to Chanel Zero," he finally said.

After changing frequency he let his hand portable radio fall loosely onto its straps and proffered Chapelon's master his hand…

The captain rushed forwards and spontaneously threw his arms around the man who had provided hope and encouragement for them over the last few desperate hours.

"Merci, Merci, Merci," he repeated, suddenly unable to formulate the right words to show his full gratitude and appreciation on behalf of his entire crew whose lives had been saved.

He stood back with his outstretched arms on Roy's shoulders and briefly studied him. For the stupendous task he had helped achieve, he looked so plain and normal. Average height, smaller than the captain and beneath his scratched goggles very ordinary looking.

Roy was economically modest in his reply, simply saying it was his job, before welcoming him to England and wishing him the compliments of the season. The captain chuckled as Roy drew him towards the dunes, saying that what he really wanted was a coffee and a sandwich. He cordially invited Chapelon's master to join him. Once in Druridge Bay's natural shelter he gestured towards the weather-beaten figure of Blyth auxiliary in charge, introducing him as 'Le Directeur de Suavatage'.

Blyth instantly became all smiles, pumping the master's hand with vigour.

"Director eh!" he suddenly quipped. "Do you think the DC will pay me accordingly?"

Roy laughed companionably, relieving his own tension that had been building over the last few hours.

"What do you think? But for my part, thanks. Everybody made a good choice with you."

Before he could acknowledge the warm and genuine compliment, Blyth nodded towards the district controller who was making his way over towards them, with his cap very firmly in place.

Knowing how his DC ticked, Roy waited for the right moment, before announcing, "Commodore, Le Commandant de Tyne Tees Coastguard!"

The master studied the lines of strain and weariness around the district controller's eyes and noted the 'scrambled egg' on his cap peak. He spoke with feeling when he said he could not find the words to thank him enough for the massive effort that had saved both him and his crew.

The DC understood the gist of the words and nodded formally. He glanced over at Roy and smiled approvingly. The introduction had been perfect.

"I'll take the old man over to the WRVS truck for a snack," continued Roy. "How about a break for the boys too, before we dismantle the gear?"

He was looking towards Blyth auxiliary in charge, as he spoke. The DC nodded briefly. It was a good idea, but he said he wanted the men to do it in relays.

Others could at least start the long task of retrieval and stowage.

Roy and Chapelon's captain walked together, strolling in genuine companionship through the accumulated rescue clutter now they were sheltered against the worst of the storm. The captain suddenly felt surreal, as if he was walking through a dream. He was surrounded by many willing men with their piles of equipment and could sense the collective professionalism and purpose that they represented. Feeling almost light headed he nodded and waved where he could, aware of the warm and positive response from the people who had preserved his life and the lives of his crew too.

When they were just twenty yards short of the WRVS wagon Chapelon's master stopped short, instantly bringing himself to a halt. The chief engineer was leaning against the WRVS ladies' open hatch, surrounded by his engineers and chatting to them encouragingly. The third engineer suddenly burst into laughter at one of his comments and willingly shared the joke with his colleagues.

The ship's captain felt an awful flashback. He recalled the arrival of his engineering officer's wife and daughter on board Chapelon and the report of their furious argument at Dunkirk, having the impression there was something very wrong with their relationship. He had forgotten about them as he hastily completed the ship's business before they made ready to sail. The third engineer and his obvious troubled relationship with his family had even caused him think about his own family whilst on the bridge, awaiting the pilot. Now the third engineer seemed to be totally carefree with no wife and child at his side. The implications churned the captain's stomach as he felt rising sickness and shock.

Chapter 6

Man the Left Whip!

The captain was aware he was groaning as peripheral brain cells snapped into line.

Roy watched with rising anxiety as his new companion briefly closed his eyes in horror. How could he, as master have forgotten about them? Other than their arrival as they traipsed up the gangway, suitcases in hand – and then the third engineer's request about them staying on board for the coastal passage after their furious row, he had literally blanked away any further thoughts he might have had about the mother and child. He had neither spoken to them nor seen them again. While he and his senior colleagues worried about the weather, their cargo and the ship's planned maintenance, he had even forgotten to have them sign on the official ship's articles as supernumeraries. Then, he suddenly also remembered how in the engine room it had been the third engineer who had busied himself, led and then mainly directed the forlorn attempt at repairing the main engine; drawing praise from colleagues as he concentrated on that task alone, stubbornly remaining at his place of work. Chapelon's master now realised that this officer's actions, although no doubt opportunist, made ruthless and sinister sense. In desperation, he stammered out his fears to Roy about the mother and young child.

Roy looked at the master, thunderstruck.

"Ou!" He instantly exclaimed, "sur le Chapelon?"

The master nodded miserably, dumbed by the effects of rising shock. Roy suddenly looked dangerous as the strain of the last few hours caused his temper to snap. Turning violently he stormed towards the third engineer who now spotted his furious assailant who had only recently greeted him with warmth. Fear suddenly registered on the third's face. Without stopping Roy slammed his hand into the man's chest and bawled into his face, as the third engineer was pushed back against the WRVS wagon, startling the two ladies who had been faithfully looking after the evacuees. The chief and fourth engineer heard Roy's angry words and looked at their colleague in disbelief and then, rising contempt.

Startled by his watch officer's actions, the district controller started running towards him, but one of the policemen got there first.

"Now then, sir, what is this all about?"

Roy's anger was barely contained as he maintained a strong grip on one of the third engineer's sleeves.

"This – this reptile has deliberately left his wife and child on the ship!" he spat out in open contempt of the third engineer.

For a moment shock registered on the policeman's face too, but then he rapidly drew on his own professionalism.

"Leave this to us, sir," he directed, removing the third engineer's arm from Roy's vice like grip. "If there is criminality, we will deal with it," he said with assurance.

Roy suddenly turned on his heels, nearly knocking the district controller over as he arrived at the WRVS wagon. Running hard into the wind, he screamed and waved wildly and with futility at the rescue teams as they made ready to retrieve their equipment.

"Stop! Stop!" he bellowed with flaying arms, almost ineffective against the storm, desperately seeking out Blyth auxiliary in charge.

Seeing his quarry, he dashed up to him and roughly span him around. Before Blyth could even exclaim, Roy bellowed in his face.

"The third engineer's wife and bairn are still on the ship!"

Unseen, the district controller had joined them, finally catching up with the commotion his furious watch officer was creating.

"How the hell has that happened?" was his simple and sharp demand.

"It seems that the third wanted rid of them." Roy spat out at his colleagues. "I suppose I am partly to blame too," he continued, as his flash of anger started to subside.

"Go on," ground out the district controller, with new sharpness in his own voice.

"All the time I was talking to Chapelon, I only spoke in the masculine, while the French Language has an emphasis on masculine and feminine. It was how many 'men'. Maybe…"

The district controller instantly cut him short.

"You don't need reproaching for that! You held the show together struggling with a language none of us understood. It is not your fault!" he bawled, in a voice that verged on a rebuke. "We all know of strange lapses of memory and other, almost unfathomable actions that can occur during search and rescue. This eclipses all though. No blame rests with you!" He shouted with added aggressiveness in his voice, as he seemed to browbeat his now hapless watch officer.

"Do any of your crews speak French?" Roy suddenly asked Blyth.

"Ha! them!" he responded in his guttural Northumbrian; forcing a half bitter, choking laugh. "They have enough trouble with English."

"Very well."

It was the only comment Roy made as he walked thoughtfully towards the equipment dump and started to search among its contents. He had already found a short-handled axe – a hatchet, was handling a compact crowbar and was starting to consider cordage. This time it was the turn of somebody else's hand to roughly grab *his* shoulder and jerk him back.

"What the hell are you playing at?" commanded the district controller with the sort of voice that demanded an instant answer.

Roy icily met him eye to eye, preparing for an imminent battle of wills.

"Well somebody has to go out there and get them!" he replied with sharp pragmatism, "our job isn't finished yet!"

Chapelon's master, chief engineer and others had quietly arrived to watch the encounter. Her master's sick feeling intensified. He did not understand the words of the conversation, but he could guess what it was about. This same man, somebody he had been so desperate to meet and thank, was now proposing to risk his own life, thanks to their oversight. He could guess how the district controller felt about his officer going out to Chapelon. In the circumstances his reaction would have been similar.

"No!" commanded the district controller.

Roy instantly squared up to him, line, crowbar and axe in his hand.

"Well what the hell do you propose? Do we leave them out there to die? If we do, then we have failed in our mission. Not one of our people speaks their language and somebody has to go out to the ship!"

The district controller felt unnerved by his junior's resolve.

"Let the third engineer go out to them. They are his family he so desperately wants rid of," he finally said with irony.

"And what does he know about the breaches buoy?" Challenged Roy. "How would you feel if it was your family? Look, we're wasting time!"

"Your speciality is the ops room, not this. You in particular should not need reminding that one of our golden rules is that we don't deliberately put rescuers' lives at excessive risk for others."

The district controller was quoting the handbook in desperation.

"Anyway, when did you last ride the breaches buoy then?" he asked, sarcasm and pitch rising in his voice.

"Just over a month ago at Highcliffe," Roy responded with harshness. "Remember, you recommended me for the Sector Course there; the last one to use this equipment, given it will soon be withdrawn."

"What, riding among the trees in our training centre's grounds?" The sarcasm increased in the district controller's voice.

"Exactly," came back Roy in response. "And how many times did you use me as the guinea pig on exercises when I was a probationer? Remember the time you stuck me in a dry suit and hoiked me off the stern of a boat so I could feel what it was like being floated in a buoy rigged for 'A' method? I still remember the wash and the sound of the rotating props as I went off the stern!"

The DC looked around like a trapped animal with rising anxiety, struggling to make an appropriate reply to reinforce his refusal. His junior spoke first.

"I have to go out there to get them. I have no great wish to, but what other choice is there? It would be nice to do it with your blessing. The last thing I want to do is disobey you, but if I have to, I will!"

The district controller relented. Roy had a point. He was stubborn in his resolve and time was now critical, both for his welfare and for that of the souls still on board Chapelon.

"I can't direct you to do this," he finally said, shaking his head in defeat. "I can't even recommend you do it. You do it on your own volition."

"I know," the younger man said, warmth and softness returning to his voice, "and thank you. No doubt in your shoes I would have said the same."

It briefly became their own special, unspoken moment of mutual understanding and respect and theirs alone, as the two men almost became telepathic.

The DC nodded.

"Godspeed," he simply said. Roy returned to selecting equipment from the dump. "You!" the DC suddenly snarled with a touch of menace in his voice at the hapless man in charge of the dump. "Anything he needs, he takes; and make sure it is the best you have."

Roy decided to take two fresh hand portable radios with fully charged batteries.

The dump commander, after checking their leather cases, thoughtfully placed both in clear, plastic bags to further waterproof them. Roy then chose a small torch to carry in his equipment bag and a large flash light with a stocky handle to keep with him. He selected some bright orange, braided, four-millimetre rocket line to use as a shoulder strap on the big light and a goodly sized hank to add to his rising stockpile. One of the dump attendees cut the first line to length and secured it through holes in the lamp's case. Roy also grabbed a spare, tiny snatch block and a para-illuminant pyrotechnic.

"I need a lifejacket and a knife," he suddenly said, as the dump commander selected an orange, bulky, kapok, Board of Trade standard jacket and a jack-knife on a lanyard.

Looking at his gathering heap, Roy decided he already had enough to carry. Anything more he would have to find on Chapelon. Then another thought struck him as he turned to Chapelon's master, suddenly asking whether there were any children's lifejackets on board his ship?

The master quickly spoke with his colleagues who were at hand and sadly shook his head. Feeling the tension in his stomach knot again, Roy turned to his still brow beaten district controller.

"I need to take a child's lifejacket with me," he said simply. "Ask them!" he suddenly shouted, pointing to people from local villages who had assembled to watch and help.

The dump commander and his colleagues ran towards the gathering crowd.

"I also need something to carry this lot in," he muttered, surveying the haversacks and grips available on the dump and rejecting them.

His eyes finally settled on Chapelon's master's shoulder bag, stuffed with his ship's papers and instantly demanded its use.

The master nodded, finally grateful he could provide some small practical assistance to the drama his own negligence had created. He silently removed his ship's papers, putting them in a haversack from the dump; before willingly handing over his expensive, leather, shoulder bag to Roy who was rapidly showing his impatience and who then, without ceremony started stuffing his equipment into its interior.

Once more, he confronted his hapless district controller.

"I need your cap," he said simply.

"Why?" demanded the DC, surveying Roy's sodden red and white football supporter's bobble hat with suspicion.

Roy responded in exasperation, as he pulled the bulky Board of Trade lifejacket over his head and started to secure its tapes.

"Dressed like this; you, yourself told me I look like a tramp. The third's wife and kiddy are probably scared out of their wits, marooned out there on their own. They have to recognise my authority and advice instantly. For that, I need your steaming bonnet," he emphasised, resorting to his old merchant navy vernacular.

"Well where the hell is yours!" demanded the DC, his own emotions once more turning to exasperation.

"I don't know," cracked back Roy without remorse. "Somewhere at home probably. I'd wear it if you wanted me in best bib and tucker; but as you have already reminded me, my place is normally the ops room. No point in having it there."

He knew the DC was about to lecture him on his – and quite a few of his colleagues' informal interpretation of uniform dress code. He was losing vital time.

"I only want to borrow it; you'll get it back! In the meantime, borrow my hat if you want to keep warm."

"I'd rather die of hypothermia then wear that!" shouted the DC, as he reluctantly handed over his cap, complete with 'scrambled egg' embellishment on its peak. "Look after it," he said, menace returning to his voice.

Roy simply nodded and jammed the DC's cap onto his own head. Despite everything that was happening, Chapelon's master smiled. The encounter didn't need to be fully understood for its comical overtones. Ex Royal Navy, the DC was old-school coastguard. His colleague clearly wasn't. The master empathised with the DC, but the confrontation, in the storm swept dunes, could have been scripted for an on-stage comedy.

The dump commander then appeared with a middle-aged lady, clad in an expensive Musto waterproof. She was the local doctor who was more used to administering to the ills and aches of the resilient and hardy population in the near-by scattered villages then attending a storm swept wreck service. She was carrying a child's floatation aid.

"It's only a buoyancy aid, not a lifejacket," she said apologetically, "It was in the garage where we keep our sailing dinghy."

"I'm extremely grateful for that," said Roy smiling briefly at her. "I dreaded the thought of the little girl having to ride the breeches buoy unprotected."

“Take care,” she suddenly and spontaneously said with feeling, gently touching Roy’s bulky lifejacket on its chest pad, while he managed to jam the bright yellow buoyancy aid into his now bulging shoulder bag.

Roy nodded and briefly smiled, before introducing her to the district controller.

“Your professional skills may still be needed,” he said quickly. “The DC is our strategic commander; he will direct you.”

With that, he shouldered his bag, grabbed his big torch in one hand and one of his hand-portable radios in the other as he sought out Chapelon’s chief engineer. Then he made ready to return to the full fury of the storm. Gripping the chief’s arm, he climbed one of the sheltering dunes from where, when they peered over, they had a clear view of Chapelon. He had to know exactly where the third engineer’s cabin was. There was a good chance the mother and child would still be in there.

Two minutes later, thanking the chief in his own language and with a customary ‘Merci’, Roy directed him back towards Chapelon’s master and his district controller. The third engineer’s cabin was one deck down from where he would be dropped by the breeches buoy and on the starboard side. The side facing the shore.

Without hesitation, Roy then leapt clear of the shelter provided by the dunes and almost bent double, staggered towards the jackstay hold-fast, where Blyth auxiliary-in-charge was waiting. Back in the full fury of the storm, they were once more bellowing into each other’s ears.

“Ready?” he asked.

“Aye!” shouted back Blyth. “We have replaced the breeches buoy with a fresh one,” he gesticulated. “It has been put on the right whip, as before, but we have reversed it, so you will be riding the buoy facing the jackstay's traveling snatch block. As soon as you have boarded Chapelon, we will retrieve the breeches buoy and reverse it again for recovery from the ship."

Roy found himself hesitating. What would happen if the gear snagged while being hauled empty? He wisely kept his fears to himself. Blyth was the real expert with the equipment. He would undoubtedly have considered the validity of that risk. Together they moved forwards of the jackstay tripod, where the fresh breeches buoy with its glowing red riding light was seemingly patiently waiting on the ground.

Amble Coast Rescue Team and Tynemouth VLB, despite their now own taught nerves and aware of their new desperate task, waited patiently with the luff, ready to apply tension on the jackstay. Extra hands had quietly appeared to help tend and haul on the whips. A small group waited with the breeches buoy, ready to help Roy climb in. The two breast rope men, walking back as far as their leashes would allow, prepared to support Roy and the breeches buoy, before he disappeared into the abyss between Hadston Carrs and Chapelon. The district controller carefully observed everything from a short distance away. For now, he could do little more.

Roy suddenly turned to Blyth for their final briefing.

"We will maintain comms on Channel Zero," he said, "same call signs. On the way over I'll keep an eye on the jack stay and provide a sitrep about its state when I arrive on board Chapelon. I'll let you know as soon as I get out of the buoy on board. I'll also brief you as soon as I find a way into the accommodation before I enter. The steelwork might attenuate radio signals and spoil our comms once I'm inside."

"Excuse me," chuckled Blyth, determined to lighten the desperate atmosphere around him, "but what do you mean by attenuate?"

"I'll explain when I get back." Roy laughed, as he stepped between the breeches, where the buoy lay on the ground.

"Aye," said Blyth, suddenly becoming serious again. "You make sure you get safely back too."

Glancing back towards their district controller, Roy cynically added, "The DC will be grumpy about all the paperwork if I don't!"

Somehow the dark humour seemed appropriate.

Men pulled the buoy up around him, as he arranged his shoulder bag and made ready to check the jackstay with his big torch. He could feel the crotch padding press against his groin as the attendees raised the buoy and its canvas breaches tight around him, trying to minimise the impact when he alone bore the weight. Blyth auxiliary in charge quickly double-checked everything, briefly nodded and raised his bull horn to his lips. Amble and Tynemouth were already hauling on the luff, re-tensioning the jackstay.

"Man the Left Whip!" Blyth boldly commanded.

Hands already roughened and rare from the work they had previously done, took up tension. Roy started walking along the dune top, with colleagues in attendance like dutiful courtiers. Then they fell back and the two breast rope men alone carried the weight of the breeches buoy around him. Suddenly they were falling back too, and despite having prepared himself for the moment, Roy gasped as his full weight fell onto his crotch and against the inadequate padding provided on the canvas breeches, as the wind and spray drove hard into his face. He switched on his torch and began his visual inspection of the jackstay as the travelling snatch block rasped its way along, sending its own fine spray of salt and water into his face and over his protective goggles.

Chapelon's accommodation lights, although occasionally flickering, still burned bright, as the emergency generator continued to monotonously churn out power. Roy was grateful for that mercy at least. As he deliberately kept himself low in the breeches buoy, legs dangling towards the breaking seas below and with his feet getting thoroughly soaked, he felt it jerking uncomfortably as the jackstay flexed with the ship's movement.

Amble and Tynemouth were battling against Chapelon's erratic motion as they tried to maintain the correct jackstay tension. The ship was almost in her final death throes. The smell of bunker oil escaping from its ruptured double bottoms, stung and assailed Roy's nostrils. Carried by the wind and furious seas, it also streaked his goggles. Superimposed above the terrifying sounds of the storm's fury came the sound of tortured and groaning steel. He was going to have to work fast! He had already spotted the jackstay was showing signs of wear, but nothing too serious. In parts, its red outer sheath had been worn away, but the white core beneath held firm. It was smooth with no suspicious bulges; the sign of serious degradation.

"Two more rides," he prayed, "just two more rides."

"Blyth, Charlie, ten feet. Watch for my torch signal."

The transmission was deliberately short and terse. Blyth responded with a double click, no doubt bellowing at the whip men through his loud haler. The motion of the breeches buoy slowed to a crawl. Just short of the tail block Roy waved his torch horizontally towards the shore and was brought to a complete stop. He was already debating with himself. Wondering how he would get out from his suspended position, when suddenly all the cordage went slack and he was dumped unceremoniously on Chapelon's deck. As he picked himself up, he noticed the stout canvas breeches had protected him from being cut by broken glass from Chapelon's shattered signal lamp.

"Great!" he muttered to himself as he gathered his equipment together.

During his career at sea, he had been fortunate to have never experienced being on a ship grounded on a lee shore. Chapelon's groaning and gyrations seemed doubly awful and unnatural. It clashed with his seaman-like instincts and gave him a sense of deep foreboding. How long before she finally succumbed to the sea and fell apart? Marine salvage had never been his forte, but he knew with certainty her life was ebbing away. She might stay intact for a few minutes, equally it could be a few hours. He staggered awkwardly as the ship drunkenly rolled, then she seemed to lurch and the motion was brought to an abrupt, unnatural halt. There was work to do and he needed to be fast.

Roy raised his radio to his lips.

"Blyth Alpha, Tyne-Tees Charlie, on board Chapelon, breeches buoy clear. Will advise when I enter the accommodation."

"Blyth Alpha copied." Blyth's voice brought some much-needed normality to the situation, as somewhere nearby, the emergency generator clattered.

The cordage next to Roy suddenly tensioned, the tail block rasped and the breeches buoy scurried off the ship and towards the shore. Roy knew the reason why and that it was necessary, but it didn't reassure him. In the meantime, he had to get his bearings. He was one deck below the bridge and had to descend another deck to find the third engineer's cabin, where he hoped he would find his wife and daughter. At least he was sheltered from the worst of the storm on Chapelon's lee side. As he looked around, he could see that Chapelon had clearly been a neat and pretty ship with beautiful lines. Something he would have been happy to sail on himself; but not anymore. He located an external companionway that allowed him to descend a deck. With distorting frames and buckling steel, Roy had no wish to spend unnecessary time trying to find his way around inside the ship.

One deck down, he came face to face with a solid, teak, hardwood, weather door. It would be his ideal point of entry, if he could get it open. The handle at least turned, but the door itself was stubbornly jammed against twisted frames, allowing only slight movement. Roy groped inside his bag for the crowbar. The bending of the surrounding steelwork had created a gap wide enough to jam the crowbar's end in. He pushed against the lever he had created and felt the door give a little. Jamming the crowbar in further, he threw his whole body weight against it and the door obligingly sprang open. Quickly he clipped it back on its hook and cutting some of the cordage he carried, also tied it securely. He now had his means of entry and more importantly escape. Roy's ensuing radio conversation was again brief and terse, before he stepped into the accommodation block.

The French certainly do their niceties in style, Roy thought, as he looked in astonishment at the carpeted alleyway, something he would never have found on a British ship. The internal lights were bright, but with only emergency power, the accommodation was already starting to feel cold and damp.

A short cross alleyway from the door took him to the main starboard alleyway running fore and aft, giving access to the engineers' cabins. Little signs above the cabin doors indicated the occupant. 3me ingenieur was easy to locate. Roy was now however confronted by a stout, thirty minutes fire safety door. He tried turning its handle. Even that was jammed solid as Chapelon twisted and buckled. His fist crashed against the door, hammering hard.

"Bonjour!" he shouted at the top of his voice, before placing his ear against the unyielding barrier.

He detected a whimper. Thankfully at least, the door opened inwards. That would help his break-in. Dropping his bag onto the soft, carpeted deck, he reached again for his crow-bar. The door was held with vice-like tightness against its frame. There was nowhere to jam the crowbar home. He reached down for his axe. Chapelon lurched badly, throwing him backwards. He briefly yelped as the small of his back slammed into a grab-rail on the bulkhead behind him.

As the ship steadied herself, he drove his axe hard into the door and then the frame, just above its stubborn handle. Again and again he drove the axe blade home, splintering and bruising the unyielding hard wood. He finally managed to create a small gap. The crowbar end went in a little. Panting with exertion, he drove the crowbar home, using his axe as a hammer.

Now he pushed his weight against the crowbar, using it like a lever. The door remained solid. The alleyway grab-rail against which he had bruised his back became a useful, makeshift tool, as with both hands behind his back, he lifted himself off the deck and pounded against the crowbar with both feet. After the third blow, Chapelon gave another sickening heave and he ended sprawled on her carpeted deck. On the fourth blow, the door gave a fraction. On the fifth, the crowbar gave a muffled thud as it fell onto the carpet, but the door was now slightly ajar.

"Attendre!" he shouted, as he heaved himself up onto the grab rail yet again and with an exhaling, shouted roar, drove both his feet hard into the door.

It finally yielded and burst open, slamming against the side of a louvered wardrobe just inside the cabin. A woman and young child, shocked with terror, gazed up at him, wide-eyed, from the cabin's day-bed where they sat hugging each other.

Deliberately ignoring them Roy quickly secured the open door on its cabin hook. He once again used rope to further ensure it remained open, before jamming his crowbar underneath it for good measure. It was only then that he finally turned to the cabin occupants.

"Bonjour!" he shouted, beaming and grinning.

It was an act, but he had to somehow blow away their layers of shock and stupor.

"Comment allez vous?" he continued. "Oo; et le Bon Noel, Happy Christmas."

It was too much for the child's mother, who was aroused by the awful French and the bedraggled character, clad in his bulky lifejacket standing in front of them, axe in hand. At least his cap gave him some sort of credence, but the stained goggles hanging around the bit of torn towel protecting his neck looked crazy. The lifejacket fortunately hid the rocket line that kept his oilskin in place. His greeting seemed totally ridiculous and out of place.

"Who the hell are you?" she demanded in accented but perfect English, "and where is my husband?" she continued, bristling with French indignation.

Roy took a breath, allowing his racing thoughts to pause and come together in a logical fashion. The lady's English was far better than his French. All the time he had been struggling with her native language to assist Chapelon as best he could, an English speaker remained on board. Her linguistic abilities either unknown or not cared about.

"I am a coastguard," Roy said in answer to her forceful questions, "your husband and the rest of the ship's crew have already been rescued. Now I need to get you safely ashore too."

The third engineer's wife looked at him, wide eyed.

"Maintenant – now?" she asked.

In response Chapelon lurched suddenly. The whole structure shuddered – and this time the lights extinguished long enough for Roy to switch on his torch before they thankfully came on again.

"Yes now!" Roy said with sudden urgency. It was with genuine sadness that he added, "Chapelon is finished, she is breaking up on the rocks. Where is your lifejacket?" he asked to emphasise the urgency of their situation.

The third engineer's wife shrugged, she didn't know. He looked around the cabin. It was comfortable, quite spacious and en-suite. It was fitted with a double size bunk along with the day bed, which had obviously been laid out for the young girl. There was a comfortable chair and desk with plenty of drawer space. Typical for a ship, there were additional drawers under the bunk too. By one of the two curtained port holes was the third engineer's personal radio. Like most such devices owned by seafarers it had a good spread of short-wave bands. Instinctively Roy opened the wardrobe's door and found a lifejacket sitting in the bottom.

"Bon," he said in a matter-of-fact tone.

Chapelon ground and shuddered again, this time lurching permanently to port. The door to the toilet and shower burst open and was torn off its hinges. The smell that emerged provided evidence that both mother and daughter had been violently seasick.

"The weather outside is terrible," Roy continued, "there is a lot of rain, the wind is massive and the seas very angry," he emphasised, pointing to his oilskin and then at them.

The child's mother understood immediately. Her daughter was in her night clothes and she made to remove them.

"No!" commanded Roy as he spotted their suitcase and removed a pair child's tights, two pairs of tracksuit trousers and several layers of other garments.

"And you," he added to the girl's mother, helping to bundle her child into as many layers of clothes as possible.

All the time the little girl remained wide eyed and silent. Understandably, the shock of the mounting trauma had brought on her muteness.

As her mother made ready, Roy squeezed her daughter into a pretty pink coat, with white fur around its hood. Something more suitable for playing with her friends with, rather than escaping from a shipwreck in. He pulled the hood over her head and drew and fastened its drawstring firmly. Finally, he found a pair of children's wellington boots with bright cartoon characters drawn on them and got her to step into them.

Her mother too was ready. She had taken her cue from Roy as he layered clothes on her daughter. On her legs she wore tights, leggings and a pair of jeans. A quilted anorak positively bulged with the layers beneath it. The best she could find for her feet was a pair of fleece lined, suede, ankle boots.

"Lifejackets!" said Roy suddenly.

The mother looked at hers in confusion and struggled. It was a modern affair filled with expanded foam blocks. Roy made short work of fitting it to her. He quickly tugged it here and there and pulled the straps tighter. In other circumstances she would have complained about him being over familiar with her body, but not on this occasion, not for this. She watched the concentration in his eyes as he worked rapidly and competently, checking and checking again. Suddenly, despite her first impressions and previous doubts, she was grateful for his presence. He seemed to be making absolute sense out of a world that had gone uncontrollably mad.

Unable to contain herself any longer, she found herself asking a burning question that had been preying her mind since Roy had first spoken to them.

"Do you have family too?"

Roy briefly looked her in the eye. She saw impatience there, but also determination and open honesty. Something else too she realised, as she had to briefly work out what it was. Infinite understanding and compassion. So different from the far from pleasant meeting with her husband.

"A wife and two young boys," he briefly said in reply. "I would like to see them again as well, so we must hurry!"

She desperately gripped his arm.

"What of my husband?" she demanded.

Roy took a deep breath. "I'm afraid he deliberately left you both on the ship. He is safely ashore and the police are now questioning him about this. We can talk more when you are safe; but for now I have a job to do."

"Et maintenant votre gilet De Sauvetage," Roy said gently to her daughter, who was gripping her mother's leg in terror as he told her that it was her turn to put on a lifejacket.

Her mother looked up sharply with dread. Something she had never even thought about when they had elected to stay. Was there a child's lifejacket on board? Nobody had mentioned children's lifejackets, after they had decided to remain for the short voyage to Scotland. Roy briefly grinned as he went out to his bag and produced the yellow buoyancy aid that fitted like a waistcoat. His hands worked quickly and with surprising dexterity as he closed its front fastenings and the strap that snugged around its chest.

"Bon," he finally said, leading them out of the cabin and retrieving his crowbar from beneath the door, whilst on the way out. "Time to go."

The girl held back, reluctant to move. Her mother instantly swept her into her arms and started to carry her, as once again, the lights flickered ominously. They could feel the ship grinding and flexing on the unyielding rocky bottom of Hadston Carrs. Chapelon then bent and shuddered, before lurching and groaning, like a stricken animal in her death throes. Outside, something was crashing and breaking. Roy led them quickly towards the weather door leading to the open deck. He immediately noticed the crashing noise had been the forward, starboard lifeboat davit collapsing and its boat smashing against the ship's side. It was now supported only by its after fall alone.

Above them, the funnel was starting to hang drunkenly towards the port side and the sea. Small cracks were appearing in the accommodation's side and on the deck. It was definitely time to get off! The child's mother looked in surprise towards the shore, where lights blazed, with some of them pointing directly at them, on their ship.

Roy thumbed his radio's transmit button, once they were out in the open.

"Blyth Alpha, Tyne-Tees Charlie. Back on the open deck with one woman and child, proceeding to the breeches buoy."

"Blyth copied. The Breeches Buoy is with you and ready to run."

Not even a hint of frivolity from his colleague ashore. Communications were once again, terse and sharp.

Roy's counterparts in the operations room monitored and recorded, but stayed off the air, keeping their Channel Zero frequency open for casualty working only. Between Crail in Scotland and Bridlington in Yorkshire, procedures had been instigated to minimise unnecessary communications on Channel Zero.

The small party on Chapelon staggered to the companionway leading to the next deck. Roy quickly checked it with his torch beam. It had thankfully remained sound. The ladder was secure. The mother, clearly alarmed and terrified now they were exposed in the open, still carried her child in her arms. He gesticulated for her to go first, following close behind. She hesitated. Shouldn't the coastguard be leading the way?

"Hurry! Hurry!"

Roy was clearly agitated and impatient as he shoved her towards the foot of the ladder, his body pushing her as she mounted the steps; both her hands still desperately gripping her daughter. When they had climbed halfway up the ladder Chapelon suddenly seemed to sickeningly leap and lurch at the same time. The mother's feet lost traction on the slippery treads. Her child screamed and squirmed and she instinctively tightened her grip around her. For a desperate, panic-stricken moment, she felt herself falling helplessly backwards…

As he clasped the handrail firmly with one hand, she felt Roy's other hand unceremoniously dig into her rump as he steadied her and propelled her the rest of the way up the ladder. Now she knew why he insisted she had gone first. Her offended rear-quarter and another invasion of personal space was a minor issue. He had spared mother and child serious injury. Her confidence in him continued to rise. She now also knew he had so much to lose himself, but was prepared to risk everything for their safety. She finally fully appreciated that his deep understanding of ships and his ability to actively anticipate problems, before they could become critical was vital for them all.

They half scrambled, staggering onto the next deck. Behind them the emergency generator continued to throb out is power, literally keeping the all-important lights burning. At least now it wasn't their only illumination. The powerful searchlight beams radiating from the shore that constantly reflected through spray and spume, were also focused on their deck where the breeches buoy patiently waited, sitting lop-sided where it remained suspended from the jackstay.

As Roy started pushing them towards it, the mother stopped dead in her tracks, wide-eyed and briefly speechless as she stared at the old breeches buoy with its glowing red riding light in horror.

"We have to go in that?" she suddenly asked with incredulity.

Roy glowered at her.

"Yes," he said simply. "Everybody used it to get ashore and I came out to your ship in it too!"

As he spoke she felt Roy pushing them both again, this time towards the breaches buoy, gesticulating for her to let her child stand on the deck, while at the same time he spoke into his radio.

"Blyth Alpha, Tyne Tees Charlie, we are at the breeches buoy. Please slacken the jackstay, so the buoy can fall on the deck."

Blyth briefly acknowledged and the third engineer's wife watched with further incredulity as Roy gently guided the breeches buoy to a soft landing as both whips and jackstay were slackened. He didn't use his radio this time. He simply signalled with his torch when he was satisfied. The mother observed with dread as he carefully arranged the old, soaking, canvas breeches beneath the seemingly ancient cork lifebuoy.

"You first!" he suddenly commanded.

"With my daughter!" she retorted.

"No!" Roy's reply was demanding and powerful. "I understand this!" he shouted, pointing at the breaches buoy. "Do you? Your daughter will come with me."

He carefully sat the girl down against a sheltering bulkhead and grabbing the mothers nearest arm, forcibly walked her towards the breeches buoy. He managed a brief smile.

"In a few minutes we will join you on the shore."

The mother nodded, with dread on her face. His competence and reasoning were unquestionable. Her protective instincts towards her child another matter. With Roy working fast she was suddenly stunned to realise he had placed her feet in the breeches and was pulling the whole contraption up around her. Without further warning Roy started shouting into her ear and gesticulated with wild urgency.

"Keep looking at the lights on the shore. Not at me or Chapelon, the shore, the shore, the shore!"

She nodded breathlessly as events overtook her ability to even think for herself.

"Blyth Alpha, one female adult in the breaches buoy. I will follow with the female child."

"Take up slack!" Roy was multi-tasking with both the radio and the breeches buoy.

Keeping the buoy high around the mother, he made sure she had a firm grip on the old lifebuoy.

"Haul!" he simply commanded, raising and lowering his torch, as the mother was instantly swept off the deck and he turned his attention to her daughter.

The third engineer's wife found herself grunting in shock and discomfort as her crotch slammed into the breeches and she felt her feet dangle in thin air. Roy's shouted instructions still literally rang in her ears as she stared intently at the lights ashore, eyes watering, the traveller block in front of her creaking and rasping, annoyingly spraying her face with a constant jet of salt water and fuel oil, as it rode along the jackstay. She felt as if she was suspended above the jaws of a bitter, watery hell. The whole paraphernalia seemed to bounce and flex as she was dragged jerkily towards the shore. Savage surf and sea hissed against her feet and legs, as now clear of the shelter in the lee of the ship, she started to feel the full fury of the storm on her back.

The jackstay suddenly sagged alarmingly. Icy waves swept up to her thighs as she gripped the lifebuoy with frozen, terrified hands and intently stared at the brightening shore lights with fatigued, gritty eyes.

She felt herself rising clear of the sea as the breeches buoy passed the jackstay's mid-point. Two vague figures, silhouetted in front of the lights ahead seemed to be reaching out to her as she continued towards the shore. They began to take on positive substance. A few more creaking yards and she realised they were tethered to safety lines and were wearing goggles, like the ones the coastguard had draped around his neck on Chapelon. As she approached closer, she saw their faces were swathed in scarves as protection against the flying sand and spray being driven straight into them. Their oilskins were gloss black, similar to the one Roy was wearing and around their waists were broad, blue, harnesses. They were straining hard, arms outstretched, reaching desperately for her. Suddenly, just as her feet felt firm ground, they were grabbing the breeches buoy and steadying her as they walked her back to the tripod. Only then, did they let the breeches buoy fall to her ankles, as they continued to grip her arms. More people appeared, who grabbed her and started to usher her back towards the safety of the dunes. It all seemed like an awful nightmare that she would awaken from, with her daughter safe, beside her.

Surrounded by these strangers and their confusing equipment, she suddenly and stubbornly stood her ground. Her own flesh and blood were still on Chapelon. Even the appearance of the ship's captain was of peripheral interest. Her daughter was going to have to ride that hell too! The whip men were already running the breeches buoy back out to the ship. She tried to stare intently into the driving sea, spray and sand towards the crippled Chapelon. She wouldn't, she couldn't move until her child was safely back with her. One of the many people milling around her handed her a sodden towel to wrap around her blasted face. He also gave her a pair of goggles so she could protect her eyes. She tried to gasp her thanks against the competing storm, before desperately returning her attention to the stranded ship in the surf beyond.

Roy spoke briefly into his radio, before turning to the terrified child on whom he kept a reassuring, but firm grip, as she sat scrunched up in her buoyancy aid and pretty pink jacket, with her back against the sheltering bulkhead. Above them, the tail block rasped and squeaked as the whips pulled the breeches buoy back out towards them from the shore. Roy tried to offer the girl some reassurance as he told her that her mother, her 'maman' was safely on the beach. He forced a gentle smile when he spoke again to say that they would shortly be joining her. The girl nodded overcome by fear, barely able to move, let alone talk. Despite being out in the open, in a winter's storm; it wasn't just terror that kept her complexion pale and her eyes dull and sunken. The increasingly erratic jerking and rolling of the deck beneath them continued to impact on her rebellious stomach and overwhelmed her sense of balance. The red riding light glowed brightly and reassuringly as the breeches buoy approached the ship for its final time. Suddenly, Roy jerked into action, waving his torch horizontally, while speaking into his radio at the same time. He grabbed the breeches buoy and pulled it down onto the deck in front of them as its cordage went slack. Their means of escape was at hand.

Roy ran his hand along the short length of jackstay he was able to reach and further tried to determine the condition of what he could see of its disappearing length with his torch beam. As far as he could see everything seemed sound. An awful lot had already been demanded of that jackstay, despite the valiant efforts of the Amble and Tynemouth teams to maintain a sensible tension. The weight of the girl who was about to ride the breeches buoy with him was minimal, but it would add extra stress to the already overworked equipment. He reached into the now sodden and ruined leather bag he had scrounged off Chapelon's master and found the tiny snatch block he had brought out with him. He dug around for the longest length of cordage he had left; a piece of orange, light weight rocket line that was less than ten metres long and 'bent' it on to the shackle on the snatch block's arse. He then opened its cheek and snatched the little block onto the left-hand whip, before tying the end of his makeshift emergency line onto the breeches buoy's cordage. It wasn't much, but it provided something of an insurance policy should the jackstay fail. It would enable him to draw the left-hand whip to the breeches buoy and secure it in the main travelling snatch block that was currently secured to the jackstay. The 'jury' rig would then allow the breaches buoy to hang with stability below the left-hand whip.

Gently he guided the little girl over to the old lifebuoy and got her to stand in the breeches so she would be in front of him. Then a fresh problem arose. There was not enough room for both of them. Roy cursed.

"Attendre," he muttered, before reaching for his knife with which he deliberately cut the securing cords of his lifejacket.

Briefly removing the DC's cap, he pulled the now useless lifesaving aid over his head and dumped it on Chapelon's deck. He was thankful the girl at least could remain in her buoyancy aid.

"D'accord," he suddenly said, pointing towards the shore, *"asseyez vous, asseyez vous, Asseyez vous!"*

He deliberately repeated the phrase that was now barked as a harsh command, praying she would get the message to remain firmly seated and wouldn't try to squirm around when they were riding the buoy to the shore. The girl remained rigid, silent and motionless in front of him as their feet and legs shared the holes in the collapsed, old canvas breeches. Keeping his torch and radio to hand and his knife dangling from its lanyard, he threw the master's shoulder bag clear, leaving it to share its fate with the ship he had only recently and briefly commanded. It was only then that he grabbed the lifebuoy and drew the breeches up around them.

He switched on his torch that was already showing signs of heavy use. Slipping his goggles around his eyes, Roy almost reluctantly raised his radio to his lips.

"Blyth Alpha, Tyne-Tees Charlie, both of us are in the breeches buoy and standing by… Take up slack!"

The jackstay started to ease them off the deck. The whips creaked gently through the tail block. He wrapped a protective arm around the girl, using his body as a shield against hers. Using his radio was now almost impossible, so he directed his torch beam towards the shore, raising and lowering it vertically.

Suddenly, Chapelon was no longer under their feet. The shock of their combined weight falling on his crotch as they slipped deeply into the breeches caused him to gasp all the air out of his lungs. He gulped at the sodden, spray and oil laden atmosphere. The girl squealed and squirmed as he quickly and instinctively pushed her head downwards with his free hand, before using it to grip the side of the breeches buoy. They were falling a little towards the sea, along the jackstay's natural catenary, with the jackstay's traveller block rasping in front of them, spraying their faces persistently and annoyingly with a fine, but penetrating spray of salt water mixed with heavy fuel oil. It wasn't a steady ride by any means as Amble and Tynemouth struggled against Chapelon's gyrations in their efforts to maintain a consistent tension on the jackstay. Next to the jackstay, teams of men worked in a now well practiced relay on the blue whips, drawing the Breeches Buoy and its precious cargo ever closer to the shore, while like baying dogs, the breast rope men strained at the restraining extent of their leashes.

Now Roy felt the full fury of the storm slamming and pummelling his back as he leant protectively forwards as far as his body would allow over the terrified, small girl, who now, totally overwhelmed by the events of the night was thankfully limp with inactivity.

Unseen behind him, Chapelon, in her death throes suddenly lurched violently to seawards. The jackstay quickly tightened, the rapid lift making him feel heavy in the breeches buoy as it was catapulted upwards. Then it dropped in free fall, slamming his long-suffering crotch onto the breeches as it was brought up by the jackstay. He gasped in pain, holding his breath, as he felt his eyes briefly water under the short, but sudden shock. Then they were plunging towards the sea again, with the freezing waves nearly swamping them out of the breeches buoy as the travelling snatch block loosely rattled, before the struggling men ashore got the jackstay back under control. Behind them, Chapelon's lights were finally and permanently extinguished.

They were mid-point along the jackstay, where their weight had its maximum effect on its tension when Chapelon's battered keel, with screeching finality suddenly broke. The unusual and impossible stresses which until now the ship had valiantly withstood had simply became too much, as her tortured skeleton squealed and then scrunched apart, forward of the accommodation block. The ship's back had quite literally been broken, turning her into two separate halves. Aft of the critical damage, where her accommodation block was, she pitched forward violently and slammed over to seawards. The men battling to control the jackstay didn't have a chance. The critical line was both catapulted upwards and stretched to beyond its breaking point. Out on the breeches buoy Roy instantly sensed what was happening as they briefly felt weighty under the frightening, rapid lifting as they shot clear of the sea and breaking spray. The traveller block screamed in protest against the unexpected and massive stresses before the jackstay parted. The moment, when it came, was dramatic and with no real warning. Roy instinctively threw himself right forwards, protecting the young girl, as the traveller block, released of its unusual tension, sprang back at them in recoil. The breeches buoy instantly went into free fall down towards the sea. Roy literally saw a flash of light in the darkness as the traveller block smashed against his skull. The district controller's precious cap was wrenched from his head and went spinning into the maelstrom around them. He briefly and stubbornly fought encroaching unconsciousness, before they were plunged into the icy North Sea and boiling surf. He yelped as he felt his legs slam against the unyielding rocks of Hadston Carrs, before the old lifebuoy that surrounded them returned them to the surface with its built-in buoyancy.

Fighting off nausea and blackout, Roy realised that at least his torch was still working. Searchlights were already being directed down onto them as he desperately waved his light horizontally in the negative / stop signal. Immediately in front of him, the young girl was screaming and crying as walls of angry surf and thick, black oil swept over them both. Their safe recovery to the shore was now totally dependent on whether he could successfully retrieve and hold the left-hand whip. He would then need to snatch it into the traveller block through which the jackstay had run, giving the buoy its much needed stability. It was their last and only desperate chance for survival. Already his legs were numb from the freezing North Sea and his hands too were losing their feeling. It wouldn't take long for the cold to finish them both. The girl in front of him was suddenly quiet and totally passive from shock and freezing cold. That itself was a bad sign, but it also meant he could concentrate on his immediate task before the cold permanently inhibited his desperate moves that would allow them both to reach the shore. He started to pull on his piece of rocket line and the small snatch block that attached it to the left-hand whip. Unseen by the struggle in the breeches buoy and with the powerful lights that illuminated their plight, men were trying to direct the left whip towards Roy as best they could, mindful they could tangle it on the right-hand whip. Being ruthlessly thrown around by sea, surf and swell, blinking away blood from the cut on his head, Roy gently and carefully drew the left-hand whip towards their breeches buoy. The saltiness of the sea stung his scalp wound as he tried to ignore the discomfort that added to his other pains and encroaching dizziness. He gritted his teeth in reflex. In its own way it was a blessing; as the increasing pain helped to fight off the darkness of oblivion that had hovered over him since the traveller block crashed against his head.

The surf continued to hinder them, his hands grew more leaden from the icy, crashing sea. Already he had ceased to feel all pain in his legs from the numbness of creeping, crippling cold. And then, almost unexpectedly the left-hand whip and his little snatch block were in his hand. His movements felt increasingly clumsy with the encroaching cold as he struggled to secure his rocket line to the breeches buoy. He hardly felt one of his finger nails being torn open and a gash opening up on the palm of his hand as he struggled to close the ends of the split pin and then withdraw it from the snatch cheek of the traveller block. The cheek fell open. He pushed the left whip home and closed the blocks cheek again. Then, with the split pin held between gripped teeth, he managed to re-insert it. They were back in business. With his energy ebbing, and having nearly lost all feeling in his hands Roy feebly waved his torch vertically at the lights blazing from the shore…

Among the dunes and around the tripod, bedlam briefly reined when the jackstay parted. The Amble and Tynemouth teams' vulnerable hands were suddenly dragged uncontrollably towards the rasping reeves of the luff when Chapelon's back broke. The luff tackle's blocks squealed in protest, before the knot of the line that had been rove onto the luff's free end as a stopper, jammed solid against one of the reeves. Nobody heard the jackstay part out in the surf. With the strain of the luff suddenly evaporating, the Amble and Tynemouth teams were thrown onto their backsides in surprised unison! On the right whip, the haulers found their feet slipping and sliding as they fought to control the whip as it subjected them to a new unexpected and unrelenting tension. They held on doggedly, as the falling breeches buoy dragged them towards the dune top and the danger of raging surf beyond.

"Non!"

The girl's mother's scream was prime-evil, almost animal-like as her maternal instincts instantly went into overdrive.

She immediately knew her daughter was in mortal danger. In blind panic she ran over to the whip, desperately adding her sudden, new found strength to that of the men who struggled to control the reeling line.

Her awful plight and despair galvanised everybody. Re-enacting a scene reminiscent from shipwrecks of old, people from all directions tumbled out of the dunes, adding their collective strength to the whip. The response was universal; Chapelon's crew, the people from other services and casual onlookers alike, all took a grip of the sheathed line, as collectively they challenged the forces that now threatened to overwhelm Roy and the small child. More free hands directed the search lights into the surf, until they could pick out the red and white breeches buoy with its red riding light pathetically still burning and its struggling figures, constantly being swept by the sea. As Blyth auxiliary-in-charge, megaphone in hand, instinctively raced to the dunes' edge, the breast rope men caught up with him and firmly gripped his trousers waistband. Their job was to make sure he wouldn't become a casualty too. Blyth saw the horizontal signal from Roy's torch in the crashing sea and instantly regained control of the situation. He brought the brief mayhem into check. One of the breast rope men snatched the megaphone from their auxiliary in charge, to relay his orders to the crowds on the whips, as Blyth concentrated and stared intently into the raging cauldron beyond, using hand signals to direct the people behind him, as he guided the free whip towards the breeches buoy. He was determined to provide what help and assistance to the struggling people trapped in the surf that he could, whilst having to avoid letting the whips touch and tangle.

Through misted and scratched goggles, Blyth auxiliary in charge then caught the feeble vertical motion signal from Roy's torch. It meant only one thing; they were back in business. He grabbed his megaphone back from the breast rope man and retreated towards the tripod, where one of his colleagues had already snatched the left whip into its block.

"Amble, Tynemouth and all volunteers, man the left whip!" he roared. "Right whip, gentle tension and stand-by!"

Staring intently, the breast rope men signalled to indicate the breeches buoy had been lifted clear of the water by the left whip.

"Nice and easy!" roared Blyth, "left whip pay out and maintain tension, right whip haul!"

The breeches buoy was now suspended below the left whip, that had to remain tight as it ran through the tail block on what was left of Chapelon, providing vital stability to the breeches buoy as those on the right whip used all their strength to haul carefully and steadily, bringing its vital, soft fleshed merchandise ever closer towards safety. Blyth noticed his deputy was at the head of the right whip haulers, guiding his team of willing helpers outward and away from the tripod, providing a vital gap to stop it snarling the left whip and bringing all of their efforts to naught. Once again, the breast rope men, like dogs straining on their leash, ignored the battering from the storm, blasting sand and flying spray, as they were already reaching out, with their arms outstretched towards the steadily approaching ensemble of rescue buoy and its vital, vulnerable contents.

Suddenly, drained of adrenaline and strength, the girl's mother fell back from the right whip, as other hands willingly provided more than enough power for the task. She stared towards the breast rope men in mounting tension and anticipation, all of her thoughts and emotions directed towards the safe arrival of her child. She failed to even register that Chapelon's master had appeared by her side, oblivious too of the massive and magnificent effort being made by the cold, tired, battered and exhausted people around her, who were calling on their very last reserves of energy. One of the breast rope men suddenly grabbed the cordage on which the traveller block was suspended, while his colleague grasped the breeches buoy itself. The mother tried to run forwards, but was held back with a vice-like grip by the district controller. She just stared, speechless at the awfulness combined with the magnificence of the scene unfolding before her. Her daughter was motionless and covered in black oil and blood, still snuggled in the breeches buoy. Rising horror turned to instant, somewhat guilty relief when she realised the blood was spilling over her from a cut on Roy's head. As the breast rope men gently and carefully directed their old lifesaving apparatus back towards the tripod, Blyth auxiliary in charge rapidly moved in with a blanket and plucked the young girl away from the stained and soaking canvas breeches. Nobody could dispute that he had absolutely earned that right the hard way. Other team mates formed a chain, grinning broadly as they passed the girl hand to hand towards her mother. *That too was their hard-earned privilege,* thought the district controller, as the girl; cold wet and scared, but very much alive, was thrust into her mother's arms. She held her daughter close to herself and just ran blindly and instinctively, desperate to get away from the scene of danger and carnage they had all endured as her shattered nerves finally and freely gave vent to her feelings.

"Come on, lad." One of the breast rope men spoke gently to Roy who was obviously ashen, bloodied and battered, carefully placing an arm around him, as the old, stained breeches buoy folded in on itself around his feet, now both had finally made it safely to the shore.

For the equipment it had been an appropriate swan song. The role of the worn, canvas and painted cork life ring and its old breeches, stitched with sail maker's twine, had been honourable, but was now complete.

"Leave it to us now, Son," continued the breast rope man with genuine warmth and concern, "you've done enough for one night."

On legs that felt remote and strangely detached from the rest of his body, Roy managed to step clear. He saw the district controller and his exhausted, aching brain concentrated on having to report to him. Simply walking seemed a struggle. It felt surreal, as if he was walking through syrup. His peripheral vision was going dark, as he concentrated his focus on getting to the DC. He seemed to be looking down a tunnel. He forced himself to aim towards his chosen task, his legs ungainly, making him move like a puppet, until he was finally facing the district controller himself.

"Time to pack up and go home," he managed to stammer, before his darkening vision closed to a pinhole and then turned black.

The district controller instantly threw himself forwards as he observed with mounting horror his colleague's struggle, throwing his arms around him. Then Roy lost consciousness and seemed to start folding over, before collapsing. Hugging his watch officer firmly, he managed to prevent him from free-falling out of control and hard onto the ground. Blyth had been racing towards the DC too, sensing the developing, new crisis.

He also helped support Roy's now totally limp body, before assisting the district controller in gently laying him on the soaking dune at their feet.

Blyth auxiliary in charge raised his loud hailer to his lips for a final time, towards the general direction of the waiting ambulance.

"Medic!" he roared, in time honoured fashion.

Chapter 7
Aftermath

Chapelon's master vacantly stared at the untouched, quality, single malt whisky. It seemed to glisten a beckoning amber invitation in a hand crafted, sparkling, crystal tumbler as it sat in front of him, atop a mahogany desk. The local representative from the French Consulate had brought him to his home in Tynemouth Village. It was an elegant, high ceilinged Georgian apartment, set in a tree-lined avenue, sufficiently inland to be sheltered from many of the ravages suffered by the old castle grounds where the battered MRSC stood sentinel. It was a significant blessing that in the avenue where the elegant apartment lay, the electricity had already been efficiently restored. Meanwhile, on the avenue's seawards side, the village remained in storm shattered darkness. He reflected thoughtfully about the contrast of his new surroundings following the last few desperate hours. A warm, stylish, ornate and orderly room, complete with glittering chandelier. He suddenly felt almost alien to his surroundings and found it disturbingly disquieting. He then gazed at the telephone in front of him, deep in thought. Having already insisted the master should telephone Chapelon's owner, the elderly, well-manicured French

Consular Representative had kindly told him to telephone his family too.

The master sighed through waves of exhaustion now he was in the warmth of normality. He glanced at his haggard image in a mirror on the wall opposite him and briefly closed his eyes, feeling rising despair. Not for the loss of his ship, but for the image of an injured man. Somebody who had become very special during the last few hours, who had sustained and encouraged them all, during a long and desperate night. Then finally, he witnessed him being stretchered; battered and broken, into an ambulance. By contrast his entire ship's crew were all safe. Their hurt was limited to slight shock, a few cuts, grazes and cold. Their locally appointed shipping agent and the consular representative had risen to their task of catering for the crew's welfare needs, rapidly seeing them accommodated in local hotels and providing them with fresh, dry clothes. Specialist charities and welfare organisations had also been alerted by the coastguards to ensure all their immediate needs were catered for. In France, their families were being informed and kept up to date. For now, he could do little more, other than reflect that following the episode with the third engineer, along with his wife and child, that his future as a ship's captain was probably over.

The third engineer was now in police custody and it looked as if the charges could be serious. The police had sensibly removed him from the scene when Roy went out to Chapelon. Her master had felt the anger in Roy's colleagues when they had stretchered him into the ambulance. If the third engineer had remained there, the scene could have become very ugly.

His subsequent telephone conversation with Chapelon's owner in Vaucresson had been difficult and in the end, emotionally draining. Her owner was already well aware and had been comprehensively briefed about the crankcase explosion and the circumstances leading to his ship's grounding. He had already made a preliminary decision that her crew could carry little or no blame for Chapelon's loss and was particularly relieved that they had all been saved. The master had then drawn a deep breath before telling him about the third engineer's wife and child, while his ultimate boss listened in stunned silence.

Company regulations automatically allowed officers to take their wives to sea with them. They even tolerated children on short voyages. The master had been extremely busy, but his oversight regarding the two supernumeraries was nothing short of negligence. In his heart he already knew that. He finally broke down whilst describing how they had been saved from the ship and how their rescuer; Roy, the coastguard, who spoke laughably poor French, had been badly injured and rushed to hospital. When Chapelon's owner spoke again it was in an unsteady and thoughtful voice. His final instructions to his captain were to telephone his family and get some rest.

Chapelon's master now thought of his own wife and children; warm and safe in Normandy. There could be little doubt that they were worried and concerned. He also knew that they had been told he had escaped from his wrecked vessel unscathed. It was perfectly understandable that they would be keen to hear from him directly. He reached for the telephone.

From a night where he had witnessed a multitude of awful and dramatic events, one image remained seared into his mind. That of the breeches buoy returning on its final run from Chapelon with the third engineer's daughter sat in its front. Terrified, soaking, oil stained, cold, but safe. Protectively behind her was Roy. Hatless, lifejacket-less bloodied and battered. The master had watched in horror as colleagues had gently, almost tenderly helped him out of the breaches buoy, saw him walk stiffly, like an automaton towards the district controller, who then instinctively threw his arms around him as he lost consciousness. The scene was something he would never forget.

Wearily the master held on to the handset and was halfway through dialling his home near Caen, when he hesitated and stopped, before replacing the receiver. He simply couldn't talk to his own loved ones who were safe and warm. Not right now. Not until he had determined the fate of Roy, his injured coastguard.

In Vaucresson, Chapelon's owner replaced his telephone handset and sat back in his chair, deep in thought. It was going to be a busy holiday! He recalled his extreme annoyance when the telephone rang, disturbing his special Christmas party. Then the persistent, almost forceful voice at the other end of his receiver, followed by his daughter's emotions that had rapidly turned from anger to tears as the desperate plight of Chapelon was revealed. Finally, the request regarding salvage contracts and his desperate plea to the UK authorities to save Chapelon's crew. It did not need much intelligence to deduce that both he and his daughter had earlier spoken to Roy, the man who had been injured. The same individual that had personally pledged he would do everything he could to assist his ship's personnel – and had paid a terrible price when he achieved that objective.

Obviously knowing the danger, he would face, Roy the coastguard had kept his word.

Among the grimness, desperation and sheer destruction, something very special had occurred at the wreck-site; but for the voice he had only known and spoken to with anger at the end of their telephone, the results had been horrific. With a determined look in his eyes, and his lips pursed with concentration, Chapelon's owner gripped his telephone again with a sense of renewed purpose. This time to talk to friends of influence he had both in government and in the media.

At last a winter's dawn finally broke over Druridge Bay, following a long, hard, traumatic night. Huge white seas and surf still crashed dangerously along the length of the bay and continued to boil with fury over the rocks of Hadston Carrs. The wind at least, was now finally abating to the more normal severe gale that had originally been forecast.

But it still slammed hard. It remained treacherous. Like an exploding abscess, the meteorological abomination that had seemingly appeared from nowhere, was simply unable to survive in all its fury for any length of time. The cold North Sea and chilling climate of a northern winter simply could not provide it with the vast energy needed to maintain the sustained force of brute fury that had enabled it to briefly and devastatingly lash north-east England and the Scottish Borders.

Daylight also revealed that Chapelon now no longer existed as a recognisable, elegant ship. She was a total wreck; broken into three main sections and constantly battered by breakers that twisted, turned and ground her on and around the littoral area of Hadston Carrs. One of the massive masts that had supported the Stulken Derrick remained in place between Numbers Three and Four Holds. That hunk of ship at least, could still be easily identified as a piece of maritime wreckage. That same mast that had once been capable of supporting heavy lifts, now lay drunkenly, sloping at a severe angle. At least for now, it remained fixed to its deck. Of its other, twin mast, there was no evidence that it had ever even existed.

Detritus from Chapelon now littered and polluted the once pristine coastline where over the years, nature had been encouraged to flourish. The packaged pesticides, herbicides and Tetra Ethyl Lead were being relentlessly released and churned into the environment as the steel drums and other containments burst against the shore, penetrating the sand and sea water with their lethal cocktail. The heavy oil sludge cleaner from the deep tanks inflicted its toll too, scouring silt and nutrients out of the beautiful, long sandy beaches, helping to transform them into a biologically dead zone. To that was added the ship's heavy fuel oil and marine gas oil. With the furious wind also lifting the pollutants and driving them further inland, the ecologically important dunes were suffering from their effects as well. To these lethal elements were added the more substantial contents of the ship's holds – and of course the crumbling wreck of Chapelon herself. For the salvage and clean-up operation that was now going to be needed, the first task required for the recovery of Druridge Bay was the removal of visible rubbish and scrap. That was totally dependent on when the weather would eventually permit safe access. Only then could the sensitive repair of the affected coastline be fully contemplated. Even with the mixture of expertise now needed, the task was going to be long, very difficult and very, very, expensive. The ultimate, complete restoration of the area would need to be measured in years. To even the most casual of observers seeing the scene of devastation and totally ignorant of maritime affairs, it was blatantly obvious that anybody remaining on board Chapelon simply could not have survived the night.

Of the district controller's precious, missing cap, there was no sign at all.

For all of its severity, the incident in Druridge Bay had only attracted peripheral, national, media interest. Even for the local news agencies, who would otherwise have seen the incident as a headline, it was just another incident out of a night of bedlam and chaos. For them, there was an overwhelming plethora of dramatic stories across the whole region, both rural and urban. Those who were responsible for compiling and editing the news services were free to pick and choose how to fill their columns and time slots, without the need to send reporters and other staff to a dangerously exposed beach.

Not so in France. Following Chapelon's owner's telephone calls, an astonished nation woke up on this, the most special of holidays to learn of the drama about a desperate battle in a furious storm to save the lives of forty-three of their fellow countrymen. It seemed to take a hold of the nation's buoyant mood as families celebrated their Christmas festival. Meanwhile, back in the United Kingdom, the contrast was palpable. The major Maritime Rescue Centre for the North-East of England had, unbeknown to the French only recently tarnished its reputation with its policy makers. Its staff had whole heartedly and forcibly voiced their concerns when suggested changes to national plans were perceived as a threat to skills levels in the operations room. Senior political and official colleagues for now, were in no mood to praise the district's efforts. In homes across France at least, the name of Tyne-Tees Coastguard was being spoken of in awe – and for all the right reasons.

Tyne Tees Coastguard MRSC's building had not come out of its storm battering without suffering some damage. The problems were superficial though, as the building and its staff maintained its vital tasks. A number of tiles had been ripped from its roof, while the emergency generator kept up its monotonous pounding, maintaining vital services as overworked electricians struggled to restore mains power across the region. The ancient ruins of the castle and priory had withstood the test of weather unscathed. There had been no visible damage. Clearly their long-departed medieval designers had known something!

Unshaven and with red and gritty eyes, the district controller was sat at his desk in his office. His small management team were in their office too, assessing and arranging for repairs to the extensive damage suffered by their district's infrastructure. He briefly rested his head in his hands. In the warmth of his familiar surroundings, exhaustion sporadically swept over his pummelled body as if it were marching in waves. His office windows were caked in salt. It came from spray that had been lifted by the now abating storm, having been swept up from the cliff base, one hundred and eight feet below. He had been dismally correct in his forecast about one thing though. His dreary prediction that both region and headquarters would ask searching and not-too-pleasant questions about why one of his watch officers, whose place of work should have been safe and warm, was now in hospital, had come to brutal fruition. Tyne-Tees District had never been high in the popularity stakes of either of them and was for now, rock bottom.

The DC gratefully sipped at some coffee somebody had thoughtfully provided. For now he knew that Roy, his injured watch officer was in the Freeman Hospital, undergoing emergency neurosurgery. One blessing at least rested with the press. They had plenty to be busy with elsewhere overland. Thankfully, other than brief, local requests, the media had not been excessive with their demands for information, concentrating on the destruction that they had easy access to.

He glanced up in response to a knock, followed by his door opening. Jack, who had been relieved from his night shift some three hours previously entered.

"Shouldn't you be at home sleeping and enjoying a bit of Christmas with your family?" ground out the district controller, clearly showing signs of irritability.

Jack looked a little sheepish as he replied.

"I suppose so, boss," he responded yawning, before presenting the DC with a signal in a carefully prepared folder. "We thought you might like to see this."

The district controller wearily drew the file across his desk and made to open it, first glancing at Jack again, this time speaking more gently.

"I intend to shortly go to the Freeman Hospital to find out how your oppo is getting on. I'll make sure that a sitrep is left in the ops room for you for when you go back on duty tonight. Meanwhile, you really do need to go home and get some sleep. Your next watch is likely to be short-handed. Can I at least assume your Shift Supervisor Jim left after his handover?"

Jack nodded affirmation.

"At least he has some common sense," the DC breathed, smiling gently.

"What about you, boss?" asked Jack. "You look all in," he added, concern showing in his voice.

"Hint taken," said the district controller, "Once I've been to the Freeman, I'll head for home – and hopefully you will be in bed when I get there!"

The district controller's eyes suddenly widened in astonishment as he opened the folder in front of him and scanned the top of its enclosed contents. Its addressee orders had been marked for immediate fax transmission to Tyne-Tees MRSC with hard copies to follow through formal diplomatic channels. It bore the crest of the Elysee Palace and was titled 'Le President de France.' It was a letter, written in French and it bore the personal signature of Francois Mitterrand. On the lower sheet the palace had thoughtfully provided an English translation. It was a very heartfelt, warmly worded, personal letter of thanks, from a president who had deliberately broken his Christmas celebrations to ensure Tyne-Tees Coastguard was made aware of his gratitude. He readily recognised their efforts and professionalism and loaded praise on how they had saved forty-three of his fellow citizens from a desperate situation.

The DC quietly looked up at his colleague, clearly moved by what he had read.

"It doesn't get much better than that," he breathed.

He quickly pulled over a message pad, one of the inevitable CG15 series and started penning his own instructions. These were simple. Immediate transmission of copies of the president's letter to region and headquarters and to every individual in Tyne-Tees District. In the message contents section of the form, he simply wrote, 'BZ all.' The district controller wanted to ensure that everybody should be made aware of the praises loaded on them by the French Premier.

He carefully pinned the completed form to the front of the original folder with a paper clip before handing it back to Jack. With BZ he had automatically referred to old Naval Signals parlance.

"There are enough of you in there," explained the DC, waving his hand towards the operations room, "to decode Bravo Zulu for those who don't know," he said with a slight chuckle.

Broadly translated, it meant congratulations and well done, in the highest possible terms.

"Will get to it, boss," said Jack, as he too smiled broadly, having completed his self-appointed task.

He now made ready to return to the operations room.

"You are going home!" snapped the DC, "and that is an order! The duty watch can deal with distributing this to the district. By the way, you did a superb job holding the operations room together overnight. Thank you."

The words came from his heart.

After Jack departed, the DC sat back in his chair, allowing himself a few precious, thoughtful moments. The letter from the French President couldn't have been more timely. He had no doubt it would help lubricate the bureaucratic cogs he was having to negotiate with colleagues who were far higher up the food chain then he was. He started briefly reflecting about his district and how he had ceaselessly tried to defend the sometimes forthright and rebellious nature of his MRSC staff. He had always claimed that their professional skills were of the highest calibre. He had now been proven right and the head of state from another nation agreed. Tiredly, he smiled to himself. No doubt some eyebrows would be raised concerning the signal from the Elysee Palace, given it had been sent directly to his district, rather than through formal diplomatic channels first of all. The DC once again quietly chuckled. If there were any questions about that; they could be addressed directly to the President of France! He got up, shrugging himself into his salt-stained reefer jacket and Weather Guard. He automatically reached for his cap and paused. Of course, he no longer had a cap. The individual responsible for losing it was now in hospital with a fractured skull.

The results of the extreme weather and its devastating effect meant that the Freeman Hospital in Newcastle-upon-Tyne toppled on the edge of organised chaos. In its busy departments the hospital's own emergency plans had been rapidly activated, preventing its services from becoming totally overwhelmed. Spotting the 'HM Coastguard' roundels on the district controller's staff car, an attendant in the overflowing car park kindly directed him to a reserved parking space. The DC, in his exhaustion was both relieved and extremely grateful. He also felt some warm, childish pleasure about his status. It had given him access to some special treatment. He responded in kind to the nod and a friendly wave from the gentleman controlling the car park. As he left his car and stepped inside the hospital building, the contrasting warmth and clamminess felt almost suffocating as he shrugged himself out of his Weather Guard. Once again he realised a now familiar sensation, as a feeling of total exhaustion swept over him. While he waited at a crowded reception desk inside the main entrance, a porter spotting his stained uniform jacket, personally escorted him up to a busy, open public area, adjacent to where Roy's ward was. '*Thank goodness for small mercies',* thought the DC as he glanced down at the gold braid on his salt smeared sleeves. Here, amid the bustle and sometimes near chaos, it was helping him no end.

Among the walking injured, the worried and the well, he recognised a small group of people and immediately went over to talk and sit with them. All around him, many others were pensive and quiet, some almost sick with worry, uncertain about friends and loved ones who had been hurt in the storm. Minutes later, Chapelon's master, still wearing his own salt-stained reefer jacket appeared – and recognising the district controller, purposefully strode towards him with the French Consular representative in tow. The consular representative quickly and smoothly translated his stuttered, defeated utterance.

"The captain would like to know how your injured colleague is."

Intensely irritated, the district controller suddenly stood up and squared up to both.

"So would his family!" he ground out, gesticulating towards the people he had been talking to – a woman whose features were tight with strain and was close to tears – and two young boys, confused and unusually quiet with the magic of Christmas having been brutally smashed out of them.

The DC knew his voice was unnecessarily harsh, but what the heck!

This new information slammed into Chapelon's master like a hammer blow. It emphasised the impact of his own forgetfulness and negligence. Now the results faced him in a tangible form. He hesitated and stammered. His accompanying English voice cut in smoothly.

"The captain didn't realise your colleague has a wife and children."

The master went to sit with them, apologetic and desperate to offer what support he could.

The district controller formally addressed himself to the consular representative.

"Outside work, my people live ordinary lives, doing everyday things. We aren't particularly special. Occasionally their work demands something exceptional of them." He shrugged. "I was about to try to find out how my colleague's progressing, hopefully to alleviate the fears of his wife and bairns. No doubt it should help settle the master's concerns too," he added, glowering at the unfortunate captain.

The consular representative nodded his thanks, noting the DC's tiredness and understandable irritability. As a resident of Tynemouth Village, he was aware of the coastguard station in the castle grounds, but had never given it too much thought. Other than the occasional telephone call about injured French fishermen, there hadn't been any reason to. Like it or not, he was now involved in the aftermath of Chapelon and at an appropriate time he decided he would pay the station a formal visit. For now, he had no idea the French President had beaten him to it, with his own letter of thanks and embryonic plans to possibly come to visit the MRSC himself.

Scanning the people around him, the district controller took the opportunity to approach a member of medical staff who by chance was walking by, deep in his own thoughts, hands buried in the pockets of his creased white coat.

"Excuse me, sir, could you tell me where…"

The tall specialist surgeon cut him off in mid-sentence as he looked down at the stained reefer jacket and bloodshot, tired eyes, deep in shadow.

"I operated on your colleague a short while ago," he interjected. "I'm fully optimistic he will make a full recovery from his fractured skull."

The DC's relief was short lived.

"His legs could be another matter."

"His legs!" exclaimed the district controller, "what the hell do you mean, Doc?"

The internationally acclaimed surgeon winced. He was well respected in his profession and would normally rebuke anybody who referred to him as 'Doctor', rather than 'Mister'. Being called Doc would almost certainly have resulted in a very rapid and acerbic put-down. Except that earlier he had listened to an account about the shipwreck. It had been discussed by his theatre staff as they prepared Roy for his knife. They had been told the story by the ambulance crew who had delivered Roy to them. The surgeon held back with his tongue. Before him stood an exhausted, bedraggled man, stained from the chaos of Druridge Bay. Tangible evidence of what the ambulance crew had vividly portrayed. He chose his words carefully.

"I'm a Cerebral Specialist," he explained, "but an orthopaedic colleague of mine is concerned about the possible long-term effects of the multiple fractures he sustained on his legs."

The district controller looked up at him, visibly stunned.

"You mean; he could be crippled? His work demands a degree of fitness." Unable to contain himself, he found himself blurting out, "It could finish his career!"

The surgeon spoke with a surprisingly gentle voice.

"Like I said, this is not my speciality. Let's wait and see. Now take some advice off a medical man. Go home and get some rest."

The district controller sighed.

"I guess you're right. I don't suppose there might be a chance of seeing him before I go?"

The surgeon briefly laughed.

"I need to get on with my work, but I'll have a quick word with the sister who is in charge. Even I wouldn't dream of incurring her wrath by overriding her authority!"

With that, he strode away.

The district controller had voiced his thanks as the surgeon turned to leave. He looked across at his injured colleague's family, who were quietly sat with Chapelon's master and the French Consular representative. He tried to force a smile towards them, hoping it would be the medical profession who would have to discuss his fallen man's long-term prognosis with them, not him. Could he, should he, dare he, tell the whole story to the district? He suddenly vividly remembered how the Breeches Buoy had plunged into the sea when the jackstay parted, clearly crunching its soft humanity against the harsh, unyielding rocks of Hadston Carrs; and of how Roy had staggered jerkily towards him, once the breeches buoy lay at his feet, before passing out, bleeding, in his arms.

Somehow he had managed to walk on legs with multiple fractures. *"That would not have helped his injuries,"* the DC thoughtfully reflected.

"I understand you want to see your friend." The sister, whose Geordie accent contrasted subtly with the DC's Northumbrian burr, had broken his thoughts and flashbacks of the events he had witnessed in Druridge Bay.

The district controller nodded, briefly finding himself becoming mute. For a few moments, while he could not speak, he pointed towards Roy's family.

"I've already spoken with them and it's alright," continued the sister in a factual voice as they walked towards a corridor. "But only a few moments mind," she said, "he's still very drowsy from the anaesthetic, but I think he will be pleased to see you. Now don't you go dozing off in there with him," she dictated with slight disapproval at his bedraggled appearance, while they approached the door to a single side-ward.

The DC mentally noted that everybody seemed to be observing and commenting on his exhausted state. Professionally, the sister clearly saw the district controller as an equal to her in authority.

"And if he drifts off, just quietly leave him," was her last order.

"I'd like to leave this with him," the DC finally managed to say, waving a file he was carrying.

"Oh, aye, what's that?" asked the sister with a hint of suspicion.

“Personal thanks from the French President,” responded the DC with his trump card.

The sister briefly blinked at his reply but didn’t comment, as she reached for the door handle.

“Just a short while and no more,” were her final words.

The contrast with the chaos of the last few hours and the damage to his MRSC could not have been more marked as the side ward door gently clicked and closed behind the DC. Around him was ordered tranquillity; in a clean, white, Spartan room, containing its single bed. For a brief moment it almost seemed stark and unsettling after the physical and psychological strain the district controller had faced during a long – and in the end, traumatic night. A distinct smell was there too, as his nostrils sniffed the air. It was unmistakable, a reminder of the surgical ordeal his colleague had faced and would probably continue to endure with his legs. The odour was not strong, but subtle. Slightly sweet, somewhat pungent, a little musty, not unpleasant. It was the almost aromatic, clinging remnants of anaesthetic that had necessarily been administered, prior to and during Roy’s emergency neurosurgery.

Then the DC suddenly felt it again. An overwhelming surge of total exhaustion that swept over him as he took in the atmosphere of this new and safe environment. A comfortable chair close to the bed seemed to invite him to rest. He knew if he succumbed to its temptation, he would be asleep in seconds; contrary to the orders of the slightly sinister sister. As he looked down at the bed, his injured colleague struggled to clear his drug induced stupor and focused his eyes on him. Roy’s face was already showing distinct signs of stubble growth beneath his bandage swathed head. One of his arms lay outside his bedclothes attached to an intravenous drip. His injured hand too had been carefully bandaged, protecting its lacerations, following his desperate struggle with the snatch block and split pin. A reminder of those terrible seconds when the jackstay parted. The district controller's eyes fell on the lump of a cage holding the bed covers clear of Roy's injured legs. Quietly he resolved there and then to try and keep Roy in the operations room should his injuries impede his other duties. As well as his colleague's need to earn a wage, it would be foolish to ditch his skills and ever-increasing knowledge and experience in the specialist environment of his normal workplace.

When the DC managed to finally speak, his words were almost wistful, as he suddenly, instinctively said, "You look pretty damned comfortable in there!"

The district controller had to lean forwards to fully hear Roy's carefully scripted and quiet reply.

"You look knackered," he responded, with just the hint of a smirk on his otherwise ashen face.

"I don't need you telling me that too!" the district controller retorted with an edge to his voice, suddenly becoming the boss again as he stood upright.

Roy winced with pain as he managed to laugh at the DC's indignation. It helped him retain his consciousness, with stupor ever waiting in the wings, making his eye lids heavy and blurring his thoughts.

"I also lost your cap," he managed to say with his smirk widening.

The district controller stared at him, forcing his eyes to look like flint.

"I know," he suddenly said, feigning mock anger. "You and I will be having words about that!"

Roy grinned in mischief, but his gentle laughter sent more throbbing aches through his bandaged head.

"Thanks for coming," he suddenly said, becoming serious, "it is appreciated."

When the DC smiled in response, it was with genuine warmth. Those few, carefully uttered words made his trip to the hospital more than worthwhile. It also spelt out something more significant. It meant that Roy was regaining his lucidity. As the surgeon had predicted, neurologically he seemed to be coming out of his ordeal intact.

"The lads were worried about you," continued the district controller, using the bland statement as a shield against his own emotions.

"When you start feeling stronger, I don't suppose you will be short of visitors. There will be the whole district and I daresay the crew of Chapelon waiting to see you. In the meantime," he said, becoming almost brusque and more business-like, "your wife and bairns are outside, so I don't want to take any more of your time or tire you further. I'm now going to take everybody's advice, including yours and go home."

He carefully placed the official file cover he had been carrying on the small cupboard next to Roy's bed.

"Your family can look at this and read it to you."

In the bed where Roy was resting, stupor seemed to be winning its battle over lucidity as he watched Roy's eyes start to grow heavy. The district controller made ready to quietly leave when he felt a bandaged hand gently touch his own. Roy was suddenly blinking hard, forcing away the drowsiness that had so nearly overwhelmed him. He forced his mind to work and with an effort started to talk.

"Say again!" the DC barked, in response to Roy's voice that was now little more than a whisper. He had to lower his ear close to the man's lips in order to hear him.

"What happens when we no longer have the breeches buoy?" asked Roy.

The district controller suddenly jerked erect and stared down on his battered and bandaged colleague in astonishment. Beyond his side ward, Roy's wife and children were waiting, frantic with worry. With them was Chapelon's master, clearly very upset and concerned too. Yet this young man's awakening thoughts seemed to be purely work orientated! Superficially it didn't seem to make sense; but in its own strange, slightly distorted way, it was logical enough. The DC slowly and silently started retreating towards the side ward's door, his features lined in thought. Roy had touched a raw nerve that had been shared by many of the volunteers within his district. Soon, the Breeches Buoy, along with its comprehensive cordage and ordinance was due to be permanently withdrawn from the United Kingdom's coast. More robust technology was taking over and those responsible for the country's maritime search and rescue strategy had rightfully felt that finite resources were better concentrated elsewhere. Yet for all the careful planning and decision making that had gone into formulating that conclusion, without the coast rescue equipment being available, there was little doubt that Chapelon's crew would have perished.

And when the breeches buoy was gone, his own departure from the coastguard would not be too far away, as he contemplated his own forthcoming retirement.

Since leaving the Royal Navy as a communications specialist, he had for many years dedicated his working life to the coastguard and maritime search and rescue in particular. Remembering his own professional journey, he had witnessed monumental changes during the years he had spent in the service, going right back to the days of visual lookouts in small wooden huts. As his own departure from the service loomed, he had wondered and sometimes worried how the next generation would carry forward the burden and dedication needed for the responsibilities that went with their primary maritime role.

In the fury of a storm that had lashed the north east of England and in the quiet of a hospital ward, he realised his questions and concerns had largely and positively been answered. As he reached the door of the side ward, the district controller suddenly turned, grinning broadly, his exhaustion temporarily forgotten. Deliberately pointing at Roy, recumbent and injured, he spoke out with new strength and in a resurgent voice, as he boomed out;

"That, my bonny lad, will be *your* problem!"